ADVANCE PRAISE FOR *THIS CLOSE*

"Jessica Francis Kane explores the bonds and rivalries between everyday people with the elegant precision and generosity of a true master. The stories in *This Close* are beautiful, startling, and wise." —Seth Fried, author of *The Great Frustration*

"It is with great precision and skill, as well as a truckload of clear-eyed compassion, that Jessica Francis Kane reveals her characters' most vulnerable natures, as they find themselves 'this close' to being able to move on from some blow that life has dealt them. These stories feel earned, like wisdom, subtle and ferocious at once." —Pam Houston, author of *Contents May Have Shifted*

"The stories in *This Close* perform the real-life magic act of conveying both the seemingly fated and the seemingly chance nature of events. Diamond-sharp in observation, Kane also evokes and embraces the big picture, the how-life-feels part of being a human being. I read it one sitting; and then wished I had savored it for weeks." —Robin Black, author of *If I loved you, I would tell you this*

"[Kane's] stories do what excellent short stories must; they involve their readers at once. They settle in as if the characters were always there, as if you have always been privy to their secrets, their flaws. . . . There is something deep and soul-agitating at work right here, something profound being telegraphed about relationships between those paid to take care and those who pay, about innocence and dependence." —Beth Kephart, author of *Small Damages*

This Close

Other Books by Jessica Francis Kane

Bending Heaven
The Report

This Close

Stories

Jessica Francis Kane

Graywolf Press

Stories from this collection first appeared, in earlier forms, in the following literary journals: "Lucky Boy" in *Swink*; "American Lawn" in *A Public Space*; "Lesson" in *Narrative*; "Double Take" in *FiveChapters*; "Night Class" in *Post Road*; "The Essentials of Acceleration" in the *Missouri Review*; "Next in Line" in *Brain, Child*; "The Stand-In" in *Narrative*; and "Local Birds" in the *Yale Review*. Earlier versions of "Evidence of Old Repairs," "First Sale," and "The Old Beginning" appeared in *Bending Heaven* (Counterpoint, 2002).

This publication is made possible, in part, by the voters of Minnesota through a Minnesota State Arts Board Operating Support grant, thanks to a legislative appropriation from the arts and cultural heritage fund, and through a grant from the National Endowment for the Arts. Significant support has also been provided by Target, the McKnight Foundation, Amazon.com, and other generous contributions from foundations, corporations, and individuals. To these organizations and individuals we offer our heartfelt thanks.

ART WORKS.
arts.gov

MINNESOTA
STATE ARTS BOARD

CLEAN
WATER
LAND &
LEGACY
AMENDMENT

TARGET.

Published by Graywolf Press
250 Third Avenue North, Suite 600
Minneapolis, Minnesota 55401

All rights reserved.

www.graywolfpress.org

Published in the United States of America

ISBN 978-1-55597-636-1

2 4 6 8 9 7 5 3 1
First Graywolf Printing, 2013

Library of Congress Control Number: 2012953980

Cover design: Kyle G. Hunter

Cover art: "Clouds" © Jelena Veskovic / iStockphoto.com. "Color Swatches" © stuartbur / istockphoto.com.

For Mitchell, Olivia, and Simon—
closest of all

CONTENTS

LUCKY BOY

Something about New York City makes a lot of people under-stand you should try to look your best. Tourists, for example, often wear brand-new shoes and socks. They buy them after they arrive, I think, probably spending more than they should. Recently I was buying a pair of new shoes myself when I heard another man in the shop proudly decline to take his old shoes with him. "No," he said, pointing to the store entrance, a deter-mined look in his eye. "I'm going to wear my New York shoes right out that door." New York shoes, indeed. He seemed ready for a fight.

I got to New York in the early '90s, in the spring, two days after my college graduation. I had a job but no place to live, and so spent the first six weeks of my employment at a second-rate advertising agency living with an older aunt and uncle on the Upper East Side. I was their only nephew, so they let me sleep on their living-room couch for a few weeks. When I found my own place—a small studio on the Upper West Side—they helped me move in, gave me the couch on which I'd been sleeping, and said, "Well, good-bye, Henry." They seemed a little disappointed about the location of my new apartment, but at the time I didn't understand. I was just across the park.

I settled in over the Fourth of July weekend. Christina, a friend from college, gave me a list of things to accomplish. She was both a native New Yorker and very beautiful, so I paid attention to everything she said. Her list of errands included setting up telephone and cable service, getting an air conditioner, finding a dry cleaner, and buying filter screens for the windows, if I intended to open them.

"The windows?" I asked.

"Yes, Henry. Do you?"

"Do I what?"

"Intend to open them?"

"Of course. What are you talking about?"

"You'll need screens, then. To cut out the grime."

Phone and cable had to wait until Tuesday, but Saturday I was able to buy an air conditioner and two filter screens from a hardware store around the corner. That left the dry cleaner. I had never before used a cleaner regularly, but, as Christina pointed out, I had never before been the kind of man who wore a suit every day. Everything about my life was changing then, and this seemed to be signified most succinctly by my shift in laundry habits: I had never owned clothes that could not be washed with water; now I had two suits that demanded dry cleaning only. I had been a student for nearly two decades; now I was to become a professional. I had been raised in a small university town; now I was living in a city.

"*The* city," Christina said.

Christina said it would be hard to find a dry cleaner. As I explored the blocks around my apartment, I wondered what she could have been talking about. There were at least six within a three-block radius. I chose the shop on Amsterdam Avenue before I knew that what she'd meant was that the dry cleaning should, ideally, be done on the premises. Something about the little shop appealed to me, bravely facing, as it did, an ominous, fenced-in square across the street, a miserable bit of cement with one thin tree. The tree's own canopy sheltered completely the small circle of dirt the plant had been allotted, making it difficult for rain to soak the ground. A metaphor for the city's contradictions, I thought. Of more immediate importance: the shop was open that holiday Monday. I dropped off the suit I'd worn to graduation, and ticked off the item on Christina's list. Then I treated myself to an Italian sandwich from a deli near my apartment and felt I'd arrived.

But I should describe the dry cleaner further, for it figured so largely in my life at that time, in my New York transformation. In the window, framed by a strand of white Christmas lights and several surprisingly healthy ferns, stood a female mannequin. I soon thought of her as Flora because all through that summer she wore a bright floral dress, freshly laundered and pressed to advertise the shop's services. After a discouraging few days on her side at the end of August, she went upright again, modeling a turtleneck sweater and wool pants, both a bit shabby but smooth and spotless. There was something of the university coed about her, neat and dated. She stood next to an incongruous Queen Anne side table with a bouquet of silk lilies, and she faced, unblinkingly, the dark square across the street with the stunted tree.

Inside, the shop was exceptionally neat and clean. On the wall behind the front counter was a stylized drawing of two blond women striding down a well-groomed street circa 1943. It was one of those posters produced during the war encouraging women to fill the jobs men had vacated: the smiling duo, with their large, confident steps, were going places, enjoying fulfilling lives. It was hard not to contrast the optimism of the poster with the small, hot shop it adorned.

The place was run by two women who had a winning way of saying to their customers as they left, *Having a nice day.* Christina, who had not been to the shop with me, and, to the best of my knowledge, had never been to the shop, said they were Korean. It's one of those things New Yorkers know, something not necessarily obvious to newcomers. Irish cops, Filipino nannies, Pakistani cab drivers, Albanian doormen, Korean dry cleaners. It felt strange to me to talk about groups of people this way, but Christina explained it was only generalizing about their *ability* in a profession that was wrong. Koreans make *good* dry cleaners, for example, would be inappropriate. That is an ethnic stereotype rather than an economic opportunity.

I began a weekly rotation with my suits. It took me another two months to start dropping off my laundry, just a few impersonal things, casual shirts and pants I could have washed and dried but didn't have time to iron. It was a slippery slope, though, and soon I was bringing everything: underwear, socks, sheets, towels—my slow corruption giving the dry cleaning women a power over me I didn't understand.

They might have been sisters, and both seemed very solicitous about a young boy who was often there. I never saw anyone who might have been his father. The shop was open six days a week, seven to seven, the two women always busy, washing, pressing, folding. The boy, when he was there after school and on the weekends, helped sort and fold. The dry cleaning was sent out, as I mentioned, but by the time I knew this it was too late. I was committed to the shop. I was smiling at them, they were smiling back. Christina said not to be ridiculous, but I didn't see how I could switch to another place at that point. We'd been communicating in little bits of English for months. I had made-up names for them: "Braid" had one that brushed the back of her thighs; "Diamond" wore a tiny stud in the crease of one nostril. As for me, they must have thought I was an acceptable young man: wealthy enough to pay someone to do my laundry, stable enough to have a regular schedule. All through that fall and winter I dropped my laundry bag off every Saturday morning on my way to the park for a run and picked it up Monday evening when I dropped off my suit. Every time I felt guilty. I told Christina it felt like exploitation.

"Henry, *paying* them isn't exploitation," she said, and after a moment that did seem right.

By Christmas, Christina and I were dating and in the spring I was invited to spend the weekend at her family's beach house for the wedding of one of her cousins. I remember standing in the kitchen the first afternoon and asking if there was anything I could do to help. One of those questions you ask because you must, expecting people to demur.

Christina's mother, Susan, arrived with groceries. "Yes," she said. "Come wash lettuce."

We stood by the sink under a large window decorated with small vintage evening purses, little sequined clam bellies, glinting in the sun. Susan talked fast and washed lettuce faster. I struggled with the salad spinner, one that seemed to defy the laws of physics. A gentle pull of the cord and I got ninety miles per hour. I couldn't stop it, and as the mound of washed lettuce was growing exponentially on my left, I couldn't wait for it to lose momentum either. I jammed in my thumb, shook out the dry lettuce, started again. Susan chatted about Christ, death (her father's the previous spring), the prospect of the newlyweds becoming Catholic. I thought they already were.

"Lapsed," she said.

I nodded.

"What are you?"

"Episcopalian."

She shrugged, a gesture I recognized. It meant I could improve myself if I tried.

The day something changed at the dry cleaner I was standing in line behind an older gentleman. He was complaining about the troubles he'd had with his shirts, though at a different establishment. Braid was helping him, but when he went on and on, Diamond came over. The boy followed her, so finally all three of them were facing the irritable man, understanding only half of what he was saying. It seemed deeply unfair, and so I stepped in. "This is a good place," I said. "I've never had a problem."

Then I smiled at the boy.

I thought, with all my brand-new New York bravado, that I could show him not all customers were so difficult. He didn't smile back, but when I looked up, Diamond and Braid were smiling. Diamond put her arm around the boy and scooted him forward. You could see the resistance in his body, hear the soles of his sneakers squeaking on the linoleum, but the man left and the rest of us kept smiling and suddenly I felt a great misunderstanding was in the making.

Christina frowned when I told her. "Surely you're making too much of it," she said. We were on our way to my Wednesday-night confirmation class.

"Maybe," I said, but I wasn't. The next week Diamond asked me to take the boy to the park.

"He likes baseball. Good at throwing," she said eagerly. "Needs help catching."

I looked at the boy, who was standing right there. I said it looked like he had a good arm.

"Arms, yes," Diamond said, nodding and patting his shoulders.

The boy and I stared at each other. I gave him credit for looking more patient than embarrassed. He couldn't have been more than nine or ten.

"Next week," I said, turning and smiling nervously at the summer downpour that started outside just then, my immediate, foolproof excuse.

But the following Saturday I was sick and spent the whole weekend at Christina's. The Saturday after that I was back at home, with a laundry backlog. What could I say? That I didn't have a glove? That I was the only guy cut from my high school baseball team? That I throw, in fact, like a girl?

All of these things were true, but I knew what she would say. Smiling and shaking her head, *Not important.*

Searching for something else to say, I'd end up staring at that awful poster behind the counter, those happy, lucky women.

"Henry's doing something nice," Christina said at our engagement party that fall. "He's started taking his dry cleaners' boy to the park."

I frowned at her, but it was too late.

"Really? How adorable."

"Where's the shop?"

"How old is he?"

"Who do you use?"

I'd observed Christina's family and friends and the way they sometimes talked about their relationships with members of the service industry. I thought it was a way of seeming to have servants without admitting you wanted them. Mr. Greene, for example, an expensive florist Christina's parents had been using for years, was said to have been waiting to do Christina's wedding since she was a baby. "He just loves her," her mother would croon.

"We've only gone a couple times," I said.

After the party, I told Christina that I thought there were people who were uncomfortable with other people doing things for them. Regardless of payment. We were in a cab, on our way back to her apartment. She looked confused, so I tried to elaborate.

"When I was growing up," I began, "my parents bought fresh eggs from a farmer who lived outside of town. For nearly ten years this man drove a dozen eggs to our house every Monday evening, and my parents bought them because they thought they tasted better than the ones at the grocery store."

Christina stared blankly.

"There's not one story in my family about how Mr. Anderson might have felt about us."

"So?"

"Well, I'm just saying that I'm not sure Mr. Anderson enjoyed selling his eggs to us. His farm wasn't doing that well."

The cab pulled up in front of Christina's building. I looked at her expectantly, sure I'd illuminated something, but she opened the door and got out. While I was paying the driver, she thanked me for reminding her how lucky she was to have been raised in New York.

The first time I took Owen to the park, we walked up Seventy-Ninth Street. He was dressed as optimistically as Flora—a fresh white T-shirt tucked into blue shorts, white socks, new sneakers. I asked him a few things. How old are you? *Ten.* What grade is that? *Fourth.* What school do you go to? *P.S. 125.* His English was good, better than Diamond's or Braid's.

In the park, we stood about thirty feet from each other. This felt a little close, but he was small and I wasn't sure of my arm. When I threw the ball, it hit the ground about five feet short and rolled to a stop at his feet. He bent over, picked it up, rolled it back. This was our strategy because I didn't have a glove. I scooped up the ball and threw it again.

My first decent throw, Owen's body went one way, his glove another. The ball landed in the glove, but that was just a coincidence. He was a flincher. We played for twenty minutes, then I said I had to get back. He immediately slipped off his glove.

"You don't have to do this," he said as we headed out of the park.

"Do you want to?" I asked.

He shrugged. "Do you want to?" he said.

I shrugged. We were a pair.

"Do you like baseball?" I asked after a minute.

"They want me to have more friends."

A police car wailed past, allowing me to pretend I hadn't heard him. When it was gone, he said, as if I'd asked again, "Yeah, I like baseball."

Owen always thanked me just before we got back to the shop; he never forgot. Then we'd step inside and Braid or Diamond would bark at him in Korean and he would turn and say thank you again, as if he hadn't before. Something else I remember: he offered to share his glove that first day, suggested we take turns with it. I did try, but it was too small.

I thought a lot about switching shops. There was a place two blocks down on Broadway I could have gone to easily. Given the nature of the city and the hours we all worked, Diamond, Braid, and Owen never would have seen me again. After a while, they could believe I'd moved away—perhaps suddenly, for work. I would abandon a load of laundry, for verisimilitude.

I cultivated this plan or others like it every week, but by Saturday lost all resolve. An affair with Diamond or Braid might have been easier, I think. The rules of infidelity are widely known, but befriending a child?

Christina said, "Maybe they think they're helping you, have you thought of that? What do *they* see? A quiet young man who comes into the shop obsessively at the same time every Saturday, more clothes for work than leisure." She raised her eyebrows, tilted her head.

"But how did I get so"—I searched for the word— "entangled?"

"Oh, Henry, stop feeling so charitable," she said.

She came with me the next week, on a Monday, after work. Looking at her heels and very nice suit I wished it had been a Saturday, when her clothes would have been a little closer to what Braid and Diamond usually wore. The two smiled, and so did Christina, but not as broadly. With no possibility of real introductions—how could I have let so much time pass without learning their real names?—I just smiled, too, and willed the credit card machine to do its work more quickly than it ever had before.

"Is Owen here?" I asked.

Diamond nodded and called out.

When Owen emerged from the back, I introduced him. Then Christina did a strange thing: she reached over the counter and tousled his hair. "So you're the boy who takes up all my guy's Saturday mornings," she said.

He nodded.

"We are very grateful," Diamond said, smiling.

Then Christina looked at her watch.

It was getting late and we had dinner reservations, but the gesture erased Diamond's smile and sent her scrambling for the receipt when the machine finally scratched it out. To make up for any harm done, I waved from the door and said, "See you Saturday!" I felt terrible.

"Those women know what they're doing," Christina said when we were outside. "They've got you lined up as a part-time babysitter."

"Really?" I wanted to see it her way, but I worried Diamond and Braid saw me more as a benefactor—the promise of New York working for them finally. And why not? We all look for meaning, for the stories we can tell to give our lives a more generous dose of beauty and sense. The florist and Christina's family. The women on Amsterdam Avenue and me. But one feature of this kind of story, I thought, was money, and I didn't have a lot. I was spending weekends at my soon-to-be-in-laws' beach house and now owned four suits, the last *two* a birthday present from Christina's parents. But I was as surprised by these changes in my life as Diamond and Braid would have been if I'd marched into their shop and announced I was taking Owen to try out for the Yankees.

Once when it was cold and windy and I didn't feel like going to the park, I took Owen to the Museum of Natural History instead. He liked the cabinets of small fossils; the tidy displays seemed to appeal to his sense of order. He also liked the dark hall of geodes and gemstones. We took a quick turn through the avian taxidermy, which I enjoyed, then headed to the cafeteria for coffee and hot chocolate. Owen sat more quietly than boys his age generally do. He tucked his heels up on the rung of the chair, wrapped his hands around the mug, and savored his drink as if it were a gift.

This outing, as well as all the others, lasted, from start to finish, less than ninety minutes. I was sure that one Saturday I would spend more time with him, that our outings would start to make some kind of sense, but they never did. I knew I was a fraud. Every week I returned him to the shop with a fabricated sense of urgency to justify my quick departure.

There. Done.

"Having a good time?" Diamond would ask, meeting us at the door.

Yes.

"He is catching?"

Yes, indeed. Getting better, I think.

And Braid would hand me my suits, clean and covered in plastic. At first she did this with a big smile; later her manner turned more businesslike, a change I appreciated, failing to understand its significance.

My third spring in the city, a wedding dress appeared on Flora—an odd coincidence given that my own wedding was planned for the summer—and someone gave me a baseball glove.

Christina found it in my laundry bag.

"Look," she said, holding up the brown mitt.

I said the first thing that came into my head, even though I could see the price tag dangling from the wrist. "Owen must have lost it."

"Is it Owen's? It's brand-new."

"Oh?"

"Is it for you?" Christina turned it over in her hands. "Do you need a new one? Maybe they meant it as a present."

Later, over dinner, I told Christina that the exchange of services was making me uncomfortable. They'd started replacing lost buttons and mending ripped seams without charging me, and I was letting them. Once in the shop I held my receipt aloft and tried to pay them more, but Diamond smiled and shook her head and wouldn't look at me. When I finished telling Christina everything but the truth about the glove, I sighed, a release of air that surprised me with its intensity.

Christina looked at me. "Leave a couple dollars on the counter," she said. "Not that you have to, but if it's bothering you just leave a tip or something."

"I know, I thought of that," I said, covering my astonishment that I had never thought of that.

"We're moving soon anyway."

"But what do I do with the glove?"

"Give it to Owen, then everybody's happy."

I must have still looked worried.

"He'll be fine," she said, her tone a New York blend of comfort and dismissal. "His mother has a job. He's in school. There are plenty of other things to worry about."

Two years and one week in the city, and this made sense to me.

I went to the shop at a time when I was sure Owen would be at school. When Diamond and Braid saw me, they looked surprised, even a bit flustered, as if they counted on me to be reliable in my habits and were inconvenienced by this display of irregularity. New Yorkers in their way, too, I suppose. Diamond glanced at the clock. Braid started thumbing through the tickets, checking to see if I was expecting my suits early this week. I put the glove on the counter and apologized. I told them I couldn't accept it.

Diamond stared. "I don't understand," she said. And it was clear she was telling the truth; she didn't know about the glove. Braid did.

"I'm giving this back. I don't need it." I meant I didn't want it, but I backed away from the stronger word.

"No more playing without," Braid said firmly, then turned and spoke to Diamond in Korean.

"You don't have a glove?" Diamond said, pointing to the glove but looking at me.

I shook my head.

"But how can you—" she began.

I reminded them that it was Owen's catching we were supposed to be working on, and I defended my approach even as it disgusted me. Worse, I spoke to them as if I was explaining something obvious, something obvious to Americans.

"I didn't know," Diamond said quietly.

Braid did not speak. She watched me while I was speaking—I could see her jaw twitching—then she turned and walked to the back of the shop. Owen was smart to confide in her, I thought. She'll keep him safe, though Diamond was probably his mother.

Diamond remained at the counter, fingering the glove as if it were lace. I believed I was only returning a gift, not ending my relationship with Owen, but I never went back. A few months later, Christina and I moved to the Upper East Side.

"I'm sorry," I said, and plunked down fifty dollars for all the buttons and seams and lopsided fairness. I felt myself bowing slightly as I backed out of the shop.

Some people are meant to be in New York and they find a way to live here that works for them. You make decisions. Are you going to take the subway after midnight or not? Are you going to give money to panhandlers or not? You've got to have a policy because you can't agonize every time. Some people complain that the city is crowded, but aren't all cities? It seems to me the very definition. Others say you can't raise kids here, but isn't it hard raising kids anywhere? The real estate is expensive, but when people complain about that what they really mean is they can't afford a better place. Neither could my parents, and they lived in a small town.

There's a deli Christina and I patronize now on the corner of Lexington and Seventy-Seventh. To some I say we're friends with the owner, but I recognize the relationship for what it is. We are the parents with a jog stroller who buy lox when friends are in town and many other specialty items on a regular basis. He is the owner who makes us feel special when we walk into his shop so we won't take our business to any one of a dozen other delicatessens within a three-block radius. We have several subjects we banter happily about, all of them more significant than the weather, less controversial than religion.

Call it a New York friendship: mercantile devotion disguised as bonhomie.

The other morning, exhausted from the temporary quarters we're enduring while some work is done on our apartment, Christina explained to our friend, the deli owner, that we're building a spiral staircase between the floors.

Wrapping our lox, he said, "You are?"

"Yes," she said, wilting to show how tiring it all was.

Something in me snapped. "Well, no," I said. "Actually we've hired a contractor who's doing the work."

It's a distinction worth honoring, I think, but the deli owner didn't look as if I'd made anything clearer.

I wonder what Owen's doing now, where he went, whether he's still protecting his mother from the disappointing natives. Heading uptown in a cab on the West Side the other day, I told the driver to take Amsterdam. We sped through my old neighborhood, but I had time enough to see that their shop is gone. It's a Mexican burrito place now, a bar with stools in the spot where Flora once stood. The square across the street has been turned into a park with concrete benches and barrels of flowers. The tree—an ash—still stands.

Christina says she's read that Korean families have huge networks all over the country and move between cities and businesses with relative ease. I believe she's right about this. But, frankly, what else could have happened? Was I going to put Owen through college? Attend his wedding? Tell people he was the boy of my dry cleaner—he's been waiting to dry clean my daughter's wedding dress for years? I can't tell those stories and I don't know any others.

AMERICAN LAWN

The white paper stood out among the faded posters announcing diversions she'd tried in years past—yoga, piano lessons, French conversation. Many of the signs in the small foyer of the public library had been up since the beginning of the fall term; now that it was March, a red one in the corner had turned nearly to pink.

"Wanted: A plot of land for gardening in exchange for vegetables." A local phone number ran in small tabs along the bottom. There was a flourish underneath the text, hesitant and badly drawn and, in the end, unnecessary. Pat decided it must be the work of a man; a woman's hand usually lent itself more naturally to adornment.

She called the number that evening, sitting in her slip in the bedroom. David was already downstairs. She looked at herself in the mirror, at her thin damp hair, at her neck where it thickened when she took a drag on her cigarette. She was forty-eight, and it was hard to believe she'd be in the car in twenty minutes wearing lipstick. A man answered and Pat exhaled quickly. She was calling about the gardening sign, she said. Their yard wasn't big but had only grass and an old flower bed, so perhaps there was room for a small vegetable patch come spring. She hoped *patch* was the right word; it conjured in her mind the dark triangle of a woman's pubic hair.

The man's voice was not what Pat had expected. But, she reasoned, it was the voice of someone reduced to gardening on someone else's land—a fair amount of bluster was probably required. He spoke English well but with an accent. Slavic, Pat thought.

He said the sign had been up since January but no one had called. A disgrace in this land of enormous, empty lawns.

She asked where else he had posted signs.

The telephone poles, he said. The telephone poles and the lampposts.

"Well, it's unusual," Pat said. "In twenty years, I've never seen anything like it."

At the dinner party that night, she mentioned the gardener to their friends during dessert, and, for a time, the conversation centered on the Croatian refugees in town. David's smile was benign, but she knew she'd surprised him.

"Is this a good development?" he asked in the car on the way home.

"I think so," she said. She was aware of feeling a little virtuous for offering the land, for using the public library where she saw the notice, for having the courage to call.

"What's his name again?"

"Kirill." She waited. *"Kear-ull."*

Ryan and Janeen wanted a safer place to start a family, and when they saw the pink bungalow on Thomas Lane, they fell

in love. That's what they told people, anyway. The neighborhood, tucked across the railroad tracks from the university,
was modest but pleasant, with bungalows next to Victorians,
brick ranches across from clapboard saltboxes. Most of the
trees on the street were mature, with limbs wrapped in ivy
and wisteria and Virginia creeper. Janeen wished for sidewalks, but liked the low privet hedges.

"The street's got character," she said. An ex-lawyer, she
would soon be a stay-at-home mom.

"And the house is a good price," said Ryan, who'd left his
DC firm to become a lawyer for the university, a choice they
both considered noble.

"We won't be here forever," Janeen added.

When they moved in at the end of June, driving down
the main road the morning after a rain, the effect was of green
abandon. They found their own yard less charming. Against
the front porch, some privet had been left to grow huge and
gangly. In one of the side gardens, an old tree had been cut off at
a height of fifteen feet. The tall stump was covered with honeysuckle and ivy, and Janeen thought the wood must be rotting
beneath the vines. When they finished the renovations on the
house the following year, they hired a landscape architect.

"They're going to start soon," Janeen told Pat. She wanted
to be neighborly, to let her know the plans included removing
the tree stump. "I hope you won't find the workers too intru-
sive," she said.

Pat frowned. "It certainly will be less shady."

"I know. It's a big change."

They were facing each other across the white picket fence
that was officially Pat and David's and needed paint. Pat began
scraping at it with her thumbnail. Janeen, to make conversation, mentioned that she'd learned their house was a Sears

bungalow and thus should not really be pink. "Bungalows, apparently, should be painted in earth tones. I've been reading about it."

"I see," Pat said.

"So eventually we'll do Bunglehouse Gray for the stucco and Bronze Green for the trim. It should look nice next to yours."

Pat squinted at the pink house behind Janeen. "I've always been fond of the pink."

"Oh," said Janeen.

Pat squatted to get at a bit of loose paint near the ground. "How are you feeling?" she asked.

"Better now. Just a little tired."

"When are you due?"

"November."

"Be here before you know it."

"I know! That's why we're working so hard on the house."

Pat laughed. "Adam slept in a dresser drawer until we could buy a crib."

Janeen nodded and rubbed her stomach protectively. "Where was that?"

"What do you mean?"

"Where were you living then?"

"Here. In this house. David and I finished nursing school here thirty years ago." Pat slapped her hands together roughly, freeing them of paint chips, then looked at her watch and said she had to go.

"She talks about how safe this town is," Pat said to David over dinner, "how perfect and beautiful. We have crime. We have a murder or two every year."

"Now you're just being perverse," David said.

"As if everyone gets to *choose* the place where they start a family. Most people just have to make do."

"What do you want?" David said. "Would you prefer they not care about the house?"

"We rented until we could buy."

"Yes."

Pat had never known anyone who could afford a house in their twenties. And already they'd added an extension to enlarge the kitchen, put in a stone patio, and rebuilt the chimney. One morning a red van parked so that its rear bumper blocked Pat's driveway, and she had to ask the driver to pull up so she could get to the hospital for work.

"What are you here for?" She'd made a stab at cheerful curiosity.

"Chimney cap. Blocks the downdrafts."

At the end of the day, the chimney was topped with a silver whirligig, a genie's plume solidified.

"They're changing it," Pat said ominously as she cleared David's plate. "It's different."

"They're go-getters."

"Go-getters?"

He'd called them the new nouveau riche when they'd replaced all the old lead-glass windows, but then backed off when Pat relished it. The next Sunday she read in the paper that home improvement was the new self-improvement. This made her feel better. She wondered what Janeen and Ryan were hiding.

In October, four men came with a Bobcat. The stump between their houses had once been a Norway maple, a tree that dies from the top down, holding on to its deadwood for a long time. In its heyday among the more composed pines and red maples on Thomas Lane, it had looked like a tree with a history. Pat had loved it, as had the Hintons, their previous neighbors who'd painted the house pink. The tree might have lived another twenty years or so if it had not been hit by lightning the summer Pat's boys were five and two. As a memorial, and to leave some privacy between the houses, the Hintons had left a tall stump and let it grow thick with ivy and honeysuckle. Birds nested in the vines. In summer, at dusk, the whole thing trembled and buzzed.

The stump was gone in a morning, and the sun shone unimpeded on the east side of Pat's house.

Kirill came to see the plot at a quarter to six, just off work from the store where he bagged groceries. He had a broad face, dark eyes, and thick brown hair cut short over his forehead. He introduced himself and shook her hand awkwardly with his left when she offered her right. They walked around to the side of the house. "So the spot is over here," Pat waved her arm in the general direction of the space, then stood stiffly, unsure of what else to do.

"How much?" Kirill said.

"Oh, there's no charge," Pat said. "I thought—"

Kirill shook his head sharply. "How much room?"

"Oh." Pat walked to the place where the short gravel driveway ended by the side of the house. "You could really have from about here—" She walked to where a tall fence ran along the back of their property, a distance of perhaps thirty feet. "To about, I don't know, here?"

She looked around the whole lot. Her colors and textures were not coordinated; none of her trees wore mulch skirts. The gardening work of twenty years was here, tangled and casual.

Compared to her neighbor's tidy landscaping it seemed a trifle, a hobby, a mess.

She turned back to Kirill. There was enough room to make a bed several feet wide, she thought, and still leave a path beside the house. "Is that enough?" she asked.

"Yes," Kirill said, nodding, but he was looking at the ground and she could not tell if he was pleased.

She wondered if she should ask a few questions, but she hardly needed references and didn't care about his expertise. She had decided to give him the land. She would use the space her young neighbors had so rudely exposed. Still, she thought something more was required, so she asked what he planned to grow. She nodded but didn't really pay attention while he outlined when she could expect produce: tomatoes as early as July, green beans and squash by August, peppers in September. She had noticed that Kirill was missing the first two fingers of his right hand. When he saw her staring, he stopped and told her quite matter-of-factly that he'd been tortured: one finger each to remind him he'd had a wife and son. Pat didn't know what to say, couldn't even seem to move her face in sympathy. He offered nothing else, only that he had come to live with a cousin in the cousin's apartment. As he left, he gestured dismissively with the ruined hand at the front yards up and down her street, all square and full of grass.

"Grass," he muttered. "Food for goats."

Very quickly Kirill stopped ringing the doorbell and began to come and go independently, as if the vegetable patch were a sovereign island. He arrived in the early morning and sometimes came back for an hour in the evening. He rarely kneeled but seemed to prefer bending from the waist, feet wide apart.

He whistled, strange melodies Pat didn't recognize, and on one occasion, she almost asked him to stop. She got as far as the window, but then she remembered his hand and could not.

There was a drought that summer, but Kirill's garden thrived. By the end of July, Pat had more vegetables than she knew what to do with. She gave away as many as she could, but still there were tomatoes rotting in her crisper. One weekend she filled a large jar with pasta sauce and took it out to Kirill. "From your tomatoes," she explained. He shook his head. She thought he was just embarrassed so she insisted, but he remained adamant. Another time she offered him soup, but he refused that, too.

In moving from city to town, Janeen overestimated the privacy of space. One night during their second summer in the house, she heard a sneeze as she left the dinner table.

"Bless you," she said.

"Wasn't me," Ryan answered.

They looked at each other. Then they looked out the dining room windows, open to the warm night, and saw David reading in his living room. While they watched, he sneezed again.

"My God," Janeen whispered, recalling the way she often talked about the neighborhood with the windows open, sometimes even imitating Pat's voice. "Thomas Lane has known only boys for some time," Janeen had repeated to Ryan just recently. "Pat has two. Apparently the woman across the street has two. They all played together as children."

"She probably wanted a girl," Ryan said.

"Who?"

"Pat. Most women do, it seems."

And when Janeen and Ryan's girl, Annabelle, was born, Pat said both her boys had weighed over nine pounds at birth. Annabelle weighed six. Pat said something self-deprecating about a hippie diet and vitamins, but anyone could see she was proud of her big babies.

"She has a way of keeping people at arm's length," Janeen told Ryan. He agreed. He thought maybe she wasn't well. She moved as if she had not always been so heavy.

But now, at home with the baby, Janeen would have liked the company of a friend. She often stepped into the garden when Kirill was there. She felt sorry for him. He was saving money to buy a car, he'd told her, and he often stared at their Camry. "New car?" he would say. "For the baby, you need a new car. Then you sell yours to me."

She noticed he was careful never to touch Annabelle with the hand that was missing fingers. They talked about gardening, and Kirill's coworkers at the store (stupid, all of them), and his cousin's apartment (dirty, noisy), and the woman at the fishmonger (she saved the best fillets for him), and the man at the bakery (he gave Kirill discounts). Kirill had a network all over town, people who did favors for him, who treated him specially for one reason or another. He spoke of these arrangements as if he had figured out how to get away with something.

"America," he sighed, shaking his head. "I am still wondering how to win her."

"Win?" Janeen said. It was a warm morning in July. Annabelle was asleep inside and Janeen had the monitor on her hip. She was halfheartedly weeding the cutting bed while he worked at his tomato plants.

"Yes. The American dream."

"No, that's not how we say it. It's not *winning*."

"No?" He looked at her as if she were a child whose opinion he would nevertheless entertain.

"No," she insisted, but her mind went blank when she tried to think of a better verb.

"Earning," she said. "No, striving. You strive for the American dream, I think."

Kirill straightened and stretched his back. "It is not about a house?" he said, gesturing behind her. "Car? Good job?"

Janeen smiled. "Well, yes, if you're lucky, but it's the trying that's important."

"I see. You are lucky."

When Janeen told her friends in Washington about Kirill, it seemed bland to tell his stories in her own voice. "Juh-neen," she would say. "Juh-*neen*. You need always to embrace the peonies." She felt irresponsible getting the accent wrong. "He's teaching me how to garden," she'd say. "He's from Croatia."

One day he suggested Annabelle should have a sibling, and she was happy to tell him she was pregnant again. This time with a boy.

"Apparently he was also a woodworker in Croatia," she told her friends over the phone. "He wants to make the baby a crib."

In mid-August, because of the drought, the town prohibited outdoor water use of any kind.

"I'm sorry, Kirill," Pat said.

"Why?"

She looked at his garden, neat and flourishing, the yellow peppers beginning to ripen on the vine. "Because you've worked hard. And now—"

"This?" he said, gesturing toward the vegetables. "This is nothing. This is . . . small."

"But you work so hard."

He shook his head. "Just a beginning."

Pat offered to shower with a bucket in her tub, a suggestion she'd read in the paper. This he accepted, and she started leaving the buckets for him on the porch. In the shower, she'd spread out her hands, thinking how the water that ran over her body was helping sustain Kirill's vegetables.

Kirill sold some of his vegetables at the downtown farmers' market, and a few weeks later Pat passed by his corner in a local dairy farmer's stall.

"Ladies!" he called as she approached, and she looked over her shoulder to see Janeen behind her, Annabelle in a stroller.

Kirill opened his arms wide. "These are my ladies!" he explained loudly to the dairy farmer. "They shower for me. Ah, but not the small one," he said, pointing to Annabelle. "Not yet." He winked at Janeen. "Americans," he said, shaking his head. "So helpful."

Pat turned to Janeen. "You—" she began.

"I give him the runoff. Because of the restrict—"

"Yes, I know," Pat said.

"What a beautiful baby," the farmer said, looking at Annabelle, then Janeen. He turned to Pat. "You must be a very proud grandmother."

"Oh. No," said Pat.

"No," said Janeen. "We're just friends. Well, neighbors." She looked down and started fussing with Annabelle in her stroller.

"Janeen's new to the street and has done quite a lot," Pat said. "She and her husband are go-getters."

"Oh, well," Janeen said. "It's our first house."

"My friends!" said Kirill. He was delighted, beaming, and when he tickled Annabelle under the chin, she began to laugh.

"She's pregnant again," Pat said, but David didn't look up from his book.

"A boy this time. She says."

David nodded.

"Kirill's making her a crib. She doesn't even know why."

David closed his book. "Pat," he said, "maybe they just like each other. Maybe—" he stopped.

"I answered his ad." Pat was quiet a moment. "We used to agree more, I think."

"Us?"

"Yes, us. Ryan and Janeen always agree, as far as I can tell."

"I want to feel comfortable when I come home, Pat. I just want things to be nice." He gestured vaguely toward the window, toward the house next door.

At the end of September, the watering restrictions still in effect, Pat came home to find a sprinkler running in Janeen's yard. Pat had missed that sound of summer since the drought, and she stood next to her car watching the arc of water shift back and forth for several minutes.

Janeen came to her front door and waved.

"What are you doing?" Pat called, pointing at the sprinkler and smiling.

"I know. I know." Janeen stepped onto the porch. "I was just letting it run for a bit."

Pat shook her head. "You can't." Up the street she saw Kirill turn onto Thomas Lane. The sprinkler ticked and whirred. Pat closed her eyes and willed Kirill to walk faster. He could not yet see the sprinkler over the privet between their houses.

When Janeen headed toward the faucet behind the azaleas, Pat crossed the lawn fast and positioned herself between Janeen and the flowers.

"Just wait a minute," said Pat, trying to catch her breath. She couldn't remember the last time she'd moved so quickly. "You should step forward—" The water arc hit Janeen across the thighs.

Wiping at her pants, Janeen said, "Annabelle's napping. I have to get back." She started to step around Pat, but Pat blocked her.

"What is going on? I thought you wanted me to turn the water off."

"Kirill!" Pat cried. "Kirill! Come here!"

He appeared at the end of Janeen's front walk, just out of the water's path.

"Janeen was watering her grass," Pat said calmly.

Kirill pushed his lips together, waited for the arc to move away from him, then jogged forward and picked up the sprinkler. The lines of water hissed on the cement walk for a moment before he switched it off.

"I was just going to let it run for a little bit," Janeen explained. "The lawn company said it's super important to get the grass established in the first year. Otherwise you can have weeds forever."

Kirill sighed, turned to Pat, shrugged. "She wants a good lawn for the boy."

Janeen was thrilled. "Aha! Your gardener agrees with me!"

"That surprises me," Pat said. She recognized her mistake immediately, but it was too late. Kirill made a hard sound in the back of his throat before he spat on the walk.

"No!" he shouted. He took a step forward, then stopped himself and was still. "You don't say that."

He raised his left hand, and with the good fingers there, pointed at Pat. "I am not your gardener," he said. He turned and pointed at Janeen. "I am not *your* gardener," he said. Then he spat again, dropped the sprinkler, and walked away, past Pat's house without even a glance at his garden, to the end of the street. He turned the corner and was gone.

Janeen began winding the hose. "I don't know what is going on," she said.

"No," said Pat. "You wouldn't."

Pat had long ago lost track of the phone number she'd originally dialed and she didn't know his cousin's name, so when the beans wilted and turned dull she had no way to get in touch with Kirill. She harvested what she could, working in the warm afternoons, but gave most of the produce away to friends at work. The rest she threw out.

Then one afternoon, when the sun through thinning leaves had the softness of light through old glass, Kirill knocked on her door. There was no greeting, just a statement. He wanted a cold frame. Parsley and radishes would do well through the winter, he said, and he hoped their agreement could continue. He stressed the word *agreement* as if he'd rehearsed it.

She smiled, but he did not smile back. "I'd like that," she said. She almost reached for his hand, but offered instead the backyard for the cold frame, where it would be closer to the house and, she hoped, might benefit from the relative shelter and warmth.

"I don't think my husband will mind," she said and was

aware of making it sound as though she were stretching the bounds of her authority a bit for his sake.

"Yes. Good," Kirill said. "Very good." He began to nod.

Pat smiled. He looked like a man who believed he was making progress, which is exactly the way she would describe it to David when she told him Kirill had come back.

And who had he come back to? To her.

LESSON

Maryanne would like her son to know she's strong. Fifteen years of keeping him safe all by herself have done it. "Mike Leary, try and get my fingers off the steering wheel," she says. "See if you can do it."

This tall, handsome boy of hers in the passenger seat tries and cannot.

Maryanne rocks quickly from side to side, proud, lifting herself higher in the seat. He will remember this, she thinks. When he's driving on his own next year.

But Mike surprises her. He reaches over fast and digs at her fingers, scratching her with his nails. An oncoming car swerves and honks. Then, as suddenly as he reached across, her boy pulls back, disowning the attempt, indifferent.

Holding her breath, she guides the car to the side of the road and stops.

Somehow she finds the strength to smile. "Almost got me," Maryanne says. "But you've got a strong mother. Don't you know?"

FIRST SALE

The little boy bumps the apartment door open with the toe of his sneaker, lets it fall back, bumps it again. It's the end of a hot summer and Mike's waiting for his mother, who has slept late. He's dressed himself in shorts and a blue T-shirt. He's eaten a bowl of cereal, mixing the last of several boxes, and watched television most of the morning. Now he calls to her, impatiently, and Maryanne comes, slowly, her head down. She frowns as if trying to remember something. While Mike watches, she stops and looks for something in her purse.

"Go ahead," she says.

He runs down the hallway. He can reach the elevator button now and so stretches up to do it. Holding this position, smiling over his shoulder, he waits for her to round the corner. He looks down at the ashtray between the elevator doors, at the butts and black stains in the white sand.

"Look!" he cries when his mother appears, and he stretches taller on his toes.

She leans over and pushes a half-finished cigarette into the sand. "Good," she says, exhaling smoke.

He pushes the button and comes down heavily on his heels. "What's the name again?"

She sighs. "I can't keep telling you. Newfound Lake."

His father left Washington a few days ago for this place where the boy's uncle lives in New Hampshire. Before he left, he gave the boy a fishing pole and tackle box. He said that next year they would go fishing together, and the boy has started practicing from his bed.

In the cool damp air of the basement, she asks the building manager, Mr. Wallace, if they can have a yard sale on the building's front walk. He stares at them. No one has ever used the front walk of the Queensborough for a sale, he says. The boy can smell his perspiration, a sharp smell like his father's after he walks home from work.

We need to pare down, she says, and it would be a shame to throw the things away. She tells him people had yard sales all the time where she grew up. Sometimes the whole neighborhood would pitch in. The boy hears her voice change tone, grow warm and more lively. He looks eagerly at Mr. Wallace, hoping he will ask her something more.

Instead, he opens a drawer at the side of his desk. "How old are you, Ms. Leary? Twenty-five? How much stuff could you have?"

"Enough," she says, her voice flat again.

"Where do you think you're going to put everything?" Mr. Wallace asks.

They'll keep everything on the walk and front patio, she tells him, and leave a path open to the front door at all times.

Mr. Wallace unwraps a piece of gum for himself. "Isn't a

yard sale the same thing as a garage sale?" he says. "You need to find a garage!" He grins broadly, and slaps the desk.

The boy sees his mother jump at the noise. "We don't have a garage," the boy volunteers quickly. He's worried about his mother and the day. She said this would be a fast stop, but he has felt it become, like many things in the past few weeks, strangely difficult.

The manager stops chewing and swallows. "Don't look that way, Mike. How old are you, anyway?"

"Five," he answers.

"Well, you can have your sale."

They settle on a week from the day, the first Saturday in September, and his mother thanks him and leaves the office. When they are out in front of the Queensborough, momentarily dazed by the bright sun, the boy says, "He was mean." She doesn't answer, and he looks down and kicks the ground. "Grandma had yard sales?" he tries.

His mother has her sunglasses on now and is lighting a cigarette. She starts down the stairs and he steps quickly after, reaching for her hand, as he often does, to remind her of him.

When he wakes the next morning, his yellow curtains are already soft with sun and the pigeons are cooing on his windowsill. He worries his mother has started without him. He jumps out of bed and runs to her room, realizing on the way that she's still asleep. The apartment is quiet. There are no breakfast noises or smells. There are no boxes packed. He stops running and walks the last steps to her door. Pushing it open, he stands in the door frame, very still. The quilt lies crumpled in a chair and the overhead light is on.

She snores softly, her lips coming apart to make a wet puffing sound with each exhale. He calls to her, twice, loudly, wanting the noise to stop.

She groans and rolls over.

He says, "I thought we were going to pack for the sale."

"We are."

"When?"

"Soon. I'm tired. I was up late talking to your father."

"You were?"

"Yes. We—" She stares in his direction, waking up more as she focuses on him. "He's having a nice time fishing. Go have cereal, Mike, and I'll be up in a minute."

"Has he caught anything?"

"I don't know."

"He didn't tell you?"

"I guess he forgot. Go on."

In the kitchen there is no cereal or milk but he doesn't feel like eating. In a stack in the corner there are some boxes his mother has collected from the Safeway across the street and Chapman's, the liquor store next door. He looks at them a minute, then picks out a small one and takes it into the living room. Standing in his pajamas, the box dangling at his side, he looks around at their belongings, at the brown corduroy sofa, the end tables draped in shawls, the wobbly bookshelves, the overstuffed chair and footstool. There is a square coffee table with a scratched glass top and a shelf underneath cluttered with newspapers and magazines. Against the far wall, his mother's upright piano stands next to a small cabinet holding the television and stereo. To his left, behind the sofa, is a window that looks out over the flat gray roof of the Safeway.

He bounces the box against his knee. He has no idea what

to pack. All of it seems necessary to him, all of it familiar and indispensable. He's about to abandon the job when his mother walks into the room. She has pulled on jeans and a black tank top; her shoulders are bony and tan. She danced before he was born and she is still very thin.

"Come on," she says. "I'll show you."

She starts picking up things. "Anything we don't use anymore and is just taking up space. For example, these coasters? We never have parties."

She twirls around with the coasters in her hand. He stares at her, then lifts the box slightly and she tosses them in, one by one, like Frisbees, each time stylishly flicking her wrist. They hit the bottom with a hollow sound. When she finishes they are both quiet, staring at the discs in the box.

She smiles at him briefly, then runs a hand through her hair and leaps to the far end of the room. She pulls the old CDs off the shelves and scatters them on the floor at her feet.

"What about books?" he asks.

"Yes," she says. "Especially your father's."

"Which ones?"

She turns and studies him. "Never mind," she says. "I can do that part. Why don't you just help me with your things. Go through your room and figure out what you don't need anymore. You can keep the money from what you sell."

He thinks about this. "I don't want to sell anything," he says.

She turns away.

"I could think about it," he offers, but she is throwing paperbacks to the floor and doesn't answer. The sunlight has brightened since the early morning and there is much yellow in it. He hears cars on the street below, and people laughing.

It feels strange to be inside, holding a box. He turns when his mother, stepping out of the mound she has created around her, slips on a book and almost falls.

She fills the boxes quickly and loosely, then pushes or kicks them across the floor. She is working hard, fast, talking to herself. The boy has been to his room and looked through his things. He has collected some unused coloring books and a few Matchbox cars he no longer favors. When he came out to show his mother, he found her throwing clothes out of her closet. He hadn't thought of clothes. He went back to his room and pulled out the red snowsuit he has worn for several winters. He folded it carefully and placed it neatly in his box.

Now he trails her around the apartment. The surfaces of everything seem bare to him, all the pretty boxes, picture frames, and vases lying in boxes or on the floor. He sees nicks and stains he's never noticed, and hollow squares of dust, the outlines of removed things. When she is working in the small den where his father sleeps, he asks once more if he can help. His mother, leaning deep into a box, tells him there is nothing he can do.

He plays by himself for a while until, overheated, the blood pounding in his ears, he stops and lies on his back in the middle of the living room. The cardboard boxes have filled the humid air with a cloying, sweet scent. He rubs his nose to rid it of the smell. Soon the humming in his ears subsides and he realizes with a start that the apartment is very quiet. He scrambles up and runs from the room, calling.

He finds his mother curled up on the chair in her room. "I fell asleep," she says when he appears, breathless, in the doorway. She blinks a few times, then pushes the hair out of her eyes. "What've you been doing?"

"Playing," he says, his stomach tight. He pulls at his pajama top, tugging it out and away from him, balling his fists inside. "Why are you sleeping?"

"I got tired."

"Why are you tired?"

She looks down and does not answer. "Are you hungry?" she asks suddenly. "Should we have lunch?"

He shrugs and they are both quiet.

"Come sit?" she asks softly and pats her lap.

He leaves the doorway slowly, stepping carefully over the things on the floor.

"Well, never mind if it's such a chore," she says.

"No, it's okay," he says, hurrying to her then.

In his room he presents his orderly box. She makes him try on the snowsuit and when the sleeves don't reach his wrists she sighs and tells him he can take it off. Then she looks at his box again and agrees there may be nothing else, but she wants to make sure. She kneels in his closet, and he plops down on the bed.

"This?" she says, stretching an arm behind her. Between two fingers she holds a little corked bottle filled with water from the place in Maryland where they spent a weekend the summer before.

"I want that!" he shouts.

She stands and turns around, the bottle still in her hand. "Oh, Mike," she says and she is looking at him, but then she isn't. He knows this trick of her gaze. Her eyes redden and she focuses on a place above his head.

"Would someone buy it?" he asks.

She blinks and looks at him. "Maybe. It's a pretty bottle. You never know what people will want."

"Okay," he says.

She smiles sadly. "No, you should keep it. They're your memories."

The bottle is made of clear glass with a picture of a crab etched into the front. His father bought it for him at a store in town on their last afternoon. When they got back to the cabin, the boy waded into the water until it came up to his knees. His parents were standing behind him on the shore, and when he'd been out there a long time they called to him.

It won't fit the whole bay, his father said.

I know, he answered.

What're you doing, honey? his mother called.

Scooping the sunlight, he explained.

And his parents had laughed. He understood then that it was impossible, to scoop the sunlight, but he liked their laughing and he liked the idea that he could make them laugh. Standing in the path of sunshine bouncing on the water, he had turned toward them and scooped and splashed some more.

Now he shakes the bottle. A bit of sand swirls up from the bottom, but the water looks dull. "No," he says. "It's okay, but I don't see why anyone would want it." He slides off the bed and puts the bottle gently in the box for the sale.

In the week before the yard sale, morning becomes night and night day. They eat eggs for dinner and sandwiches for breakfast; they are often awake at midnight and asleep at noon. They eat at the coffee table in the living room, the kitchen table too roomy, she says, for just the two of them. He tries to set their places the way she used to, scrupulously folding white paper napkins into triangles and placing the fork and knife neatly on top. They sit Indian-style on pillows on the floor.

"Isn't this more fun?" she asks, and he watches her across the table and nods.

She sleeps late in the mornings, but at night she moves about. He hears her in the kitchen, at the piano. She plays softly, humming over the notes in broken phrases. A few times he hears her footsteps outside his door.

As the sale approaches, he does everything he can to help. She says it will be fun, but he just wants it to go well. He searches his room and finds more things to sell, some puzzles and games, a few toys.

Twice the boys from the building come by and ask him to play, but he refuses. He wants to stay home. He feels vigilant, brave, necessary. It is early September, the days already shorter and the apartment, much to his consternation, always in dim half light. He walks from room to room in the early evening while his mother sleeps, turning lights on everywhere, trying to banish with electric light whatever it is that is making her sad.

"Negotiate anything, get rid of everything. That will be the motto of the day," she says cheerfully, holding a pen in her mouth while she peels off a sticker. It is the day of the sale and she has brushed her hair and pulled it back into a soft fresh ponytail. She was up this morning before him and he thinks she looks wonderful. When she sees him looking at her, she explains that *negotiate* means being willing to compromise.

"You're only five," she says. "You probably don't know that word yet."

He nods gravely and returns to his work.

Flanked by two rectangular patches of lawn, the front walk is five sidewalk squares across by eight squares deep.

In the center, three steps lead up to a narrow patio and the Queensborough's front door. Carpeted in bright green plastic, the patio runs the width of the walk and is as high as the boy's waist. On this ledge he sets in decreasing size from left to right several pairs of old shoes, starting with a pair of his father's and finishing with his own winter boots. In between are a couple pairs of his mother's shiny heels. She waits patiently for him to finish, her hand on her hip, a funny smile on her face.

"They look great," she says when he is done, and she tousles his hair. "Now help me with the other things."

They spread an old blanket on the right side of the walk, and although the morning is still and hot, he anchors every corner with rocks from his collection. They fold the clothing in neat rows and set out the other small items, all labeled now with prices. The furniture stands in a row on the opposite side of the walk, leaving a path open, as promised, to the steps and the front door.

When everything is ready, they sit on the patio ledge next to the shoes and survey the scene. The whole area shimmers in bright morning sun. Pots of pink and red geraniums at either end of the patio fill the area with a humid fragrance. The boy doesn't know where all these things from his home have been kept, but now, arranged in this way in the open air and sunshine, they look fine to him. It is nine o'clock, and people are beginning to move about the neighborhood. An old man pushes his shopping cart toward the Safeway; Mr. Cusano, the owner of the café across the street, comes out and with a great clanging lifts the metal awning that covers his storefront at night. As he turns to go in, he waves to the boy.

"You know him?" his mother asks.

"Yes," he answers, feeling important.

He looks at his mother and thinks about the course of the

day, how the whole of it will be spent in this space. He's relieved to be out of the apartment, relieved that she seems happy. Even though they can run upstairs if they have to, she has said they should make it feel like a day out, like an adventure. She has packed a lunch for them, and a bag of things to do.

By the time the cicadas start, filling the damp air with the sound of heat, the sale has been going an hour and a half. They have sold nothing. Sitting on the ledge, bouncing his heels nervously against the wall, he watches his mother out of the corner of his eye. She reads a magazine and the morning wears on. People come and go, some stop to browse, but no one buys anything. He concentrates on every person who passes.

Then a girl walking a dog stands a long time looking at the dresser and rocking chair. When she turns to speak to his mother, the dog jumps up on the boy's legs. He starts to push him down, but when he sees his mother stand and smile at the girl, he holds the dog's paws and lets him lick his hands. The girl decides to buy both pieces. She has just graduated from college and moved to the city with her boyfriend. She and his mother talk for a while about college and moving, first apartments and jobs. Then his mother says she won't take more than thirty dollars for both things, even though the original price was twenty for each.

"Save your money," she says. "You never know when it might be useful to have some of your own."

More time passes without a sale, but the boy feels at ease. He starts a new coloring book and his mother returns to her magazine. Occasionally she gets up to straighten things browsers have displaced and gradually they sell more, his mother handling all the sales and keeping the money in an envelope in her pocket. She smiles at everyone who turns off the sidewalk, and she thanks each person who takes away something that was theirs.

At one o'clock she says it is time for lunch, and they move into the shade of the gingko tree at the corner of the building. While she unwraps his sandwich, she asks him if there's anything he's looking forward to about going back to school next week. "First grade," she says. "I can't believe it."

He feels the weight of her attention and wants to answer the question well.

"I hope the beekeeper comes again," he says.

She looks at him, puzzled.

"He came last year and told us about bees. He touched the fur on its back and—"

"I don't remember this. Someone brought bees into your classroom?"

"Yeah. A bumblebee. We could pet it, if we wanted."

"Did you?"

Remembering his fear, he looks down. "No."

She says it must have been an interesting demonstration, but he should be careful, that it was probably a special kind of bee and not like the ones outside.

"But," he insists, "he said bumblebees don't want to sting. He put it in his mouth and let it fly off his tongue." Seeing her expression, he rushes on. "He did. Just like this. Watch." He breaks off a piece of pretzel. "This is the bee," he says, cupping the bit of pretzel in his hand, then popping it into his mouth. A few seconds later, he opens his mouth and sticks out the tip of his tongue. The pretzel balances there unbroken. "That's how he did it," he finishes, chewing quickly and swallowing.

She laughs and the boy, pleased, talks faster. "The bee

stayed there for a second, and the beekeeper rolled his eyes, and then it flew away."

He hopes she will ask more questions—there's a lot to tell her about the bee, he realizes—but she's quiet now and looks away.

"I should see if he needs any help," she says, getting to her feet. "He ran by earlier."

A tall man dressed in running shoes and shorts is looking at the books on the blanket. The boy watches him over the line of his sandwich, which he holds in front of him, his elbows propped on his knees. The man picks up one of the large books and starts to open it at the same time his mother tries to wipe some dust off the front cover. They fumble and the book totters and almost falls to the ground. They both laugh, and she reaches up to tuck a few wisps of hair behind her ears. With the book successfully open and secure in his hands, the man begins talking, occasionally shifting the book to one hand and pointing at the page with the other. His mother stands quietly, her head tipped slightly to one side.

The boy finishes his sandwich and opens the box of cookies. He eats three, one more than he is allowed. A few minutes later his mother turns to check on him, and he quickly hides his fourth. She waves, then takes a few steps with the man toward the patio. They rest the book on the ledge next to the shoes and lean over it, his mother flipping through the pages now, too, talking and pointing. The boy concentrates on his coloring, leaning close over his crayon, warm and waxy in his hand without its paper. He grips it hard, making red half-moons beneath his fingernails. People pass near him and through his eyelashes he keeps an eye on the ones who stop to look at the sale.

A short time later, he wakes from a sweaty nap. The shade of the tree has shifted and he and the remains of the picnic are in full sun. Sitting up, he looks over and sees his mother and the man still talking, the book closed now and tucked under the man's arm. People are returning from picnics and pool outings, many with fresh sunburns across their shoulders and noses. Mr. Wallace steps out and stands on the corner of the patio. He looks at the sale and seems to measure with his eyes the amount of room people have to go in and out. He raises an eyebrow, first at the boy, then at the boy's mother, who doesn't notice. Eventually he shakes his head and walks back into the building.

The boy stands up and begins straightening and reorganizing. Many things are gone and he's able to fit what remains into a smaller space, hoping this will stop Mr. Wallace from saying anything to his mother. He picks up the little bottle. Pretending to move it from one place to another, he slips it quietly into his pocket.

While he is straightening, he hears the man and his mother saying good-bye. He thanks her for the book; she says she has enjoyed talking; they both say how glad they are to have met. Then, hearing their voices go quiet behind him, he turns.

He sees the man reach out and touch his mother's arm. He sees her smile and blush and look down.

The boy plucks at the green plastic carpet, his chin propped on his knee. Sitting on the far side of the patio, he is away from the shoes, away from the sale. When the runner is gone, however, his mother comes over. "How's the sleepyhead?" she asks, sitting down next to him.

He doesn't look at her, but a question rushes fiercely out of him. "Do you know him?"

"That man I was talking to? No, I just met him today. He bought one of my favorite dance books."

"You didn't finish your lunch," he says, looking up, not able to stop now, his throat hot and tight.

"I wasn't that hungry," she says softly. "You did a good job, though. I saw you."

He shakes his head. "I had four cookies."

"That's okay. Today's special."

She smiles at him, her eyes sparkling. Her bangs are curly and damp around her face, her cheeks rosy with sun.

"Why is it special? Why do people have sales?"

"Oh, lots of reasons. To make a little money, to clear out old things. It's a way of starting over, honey." She puts her arm around his shoulders and tries to pull him close, but he resists.

He turns from her and stares at the geraniums, at a bumblebee moving among the blooms. "Look," he says quickly, and, almost without thinking, reaches out and touches the yellow and black fuzz. The bee moves under his finger and the pitch of the buzzing deepens. He pulls back and the bee flies to another flower farther away. The boy turns to his mother, full of pride, his eyes wide.

"Be careful, Mike," she says. "I don't want you to get hurt."

The sun drops behind the Queensborough and the shadow of the building begins to creep over the walk. He looks around at the last of their sale, wanting everything back. The dresser, the picture frames, the puzzles, the clothes—all of it came from the time before, when the days were brighter and different and his father was home. He closes his hand over the bottle in his pocket. He wants to tell her he kept it, but just then she takes his other hand and lifts it into her lap.

"My brave boy," she says and begins stroking the soft underside of his forearm in a long line from his elbow to his wrist. It tickles and he likes it, but she doesn't seem to notice and then she stops.

DOUBLE TAKE

Six weeks after his college roommate died, Ben thought he saw him in London: the square jaw and pale skin, the round eyes and devilish grin. Ben followed the man for half a block, but it was only a stranger in the crowd on Oxford Street. In the weeks that followed, Ben saw lots of people who reminded him of Mike Leary. It seemed the city was suddenly populated with dozens of men who shared his fondness for gray parkas, cheap tight jeans, baseball caps, and bargain boots.

Of course, Ben didn't know if these items were still in Mike's wardrobe when he died. He hadn't seen him for two years when he got word that Mike had drowned off the coast of Fire Island. He was remembering him as he'd looked at Yale.

Ben flew in from London for the memorial service in New York. He couldn't take any time off, but with the time difference he was able to make the trip work. He left Heathrow early Saturday morning and arrived in the city an hour before the service Saturday afternoon. That evening a few of his college friends took Mike's mother, Maryanne, out for dinner—he remembered a quiet Italian place—then Sunday he woke up early, had brunch with friends, and caught a late-afternoon flight back to London. There was a mishap with the car service and he rode to LaGuardia in a long white limo only perfunctorily cleaned from its stag party service the night before. Back in London, he took a cab straight to work. It was a whirlwind, but he was glad he'd gone.

Ben told himself the sightings in London were a symptom of his grief. Mistaking a stranger for someone you once knew well, someone with whom you'd spent those carefree, heady years of youth, must be common after a death. After college, Mike had gone to law school, then started work at a firm in New York. He'd been there three years and was doing well, loved unabashedly the money and the lifestyle. Most of Ben's friends talked of getting out, doing something else. Academia? Politics? Maybe a smaller firm somewhere else? Mike was aiming for partner and enjoying every penny. His first year as an associate, he bought his mother a car.

There was something refreshing about having Mike for a friend. You didn't have to feel bad talking about your salary because there was Mike bragging about his. You didn't have to hide the fact that you were thinking about buying a condo at the beach because there was Mike showing you pictures of his. He was eccentric and wacky, fun to be around, and you couldn't fault his love of money because he hadn't had much growing up. He was the only person Ben had known at Yale on a full scholarship. In those years, Ben said often, "I'm just glad there are still people like him here," when what he meant was that he was glad he'd met him, for a lot of reasons, but foremost among them the idea that it distinguished him, Ben, in some way. It made him seem more remarkable in his choice of friends. Also, Mike was gay.

But Ben didn't know that at Yale. Mike came out after-ward, in New York, during a reputedly wild time while he waited tables and applied to law schools. Ben was at the London School of Economics then. When Mike went to Harvard the following year, he settled down to his studies and worked actively for Lambda Legal. What had started as a rowdy coming-out party turned more thoughtful and productive. He made law review and when he graduated was offered the job of his dreams in New York. He lived with his on-again-off-again boyfriend, Alex, in a big apartment downtown. He was happy. He was a black-and-white movie made over in Technicolor. He was a years-dormant Christmas cactus suddenly in bloom. He worked long hours, but still had time for a book club. He was reading fiction for the first time, he told friends, after far too much case law. He became something of an evangelist for fiction, in fact, and started giving all his friends extravagant gift certificates to Barnes & Noble.

Then, in his fourth year at the firm, he took two weeks off at the end of August and rented a house on Fire Island with a group of friends. Two weeks was the longest vacation Mike had ever had. At the end of the first week, he called his mother, Maryanne, and told her he was having the time of his life. He wanted to do this again next year and bring her out for part of it. She was thrilled he was so happy. The next afternoon he went swimming and was pulled out to sea by a riptide. It took lifeguards three hours to recover his body.

Many of these details Ben learned while he stood in the lobby of the funeral home on Madison Avenue before the service that warm September Saturday. He was looking for a place to stash his suitcase and people were saying the body was in good shape; it was nice to be able to say good-bye. Perhaps it was the jet lag, but Ben never realized they were talking

about an open casket in another room and so he never went
to see it. Later, when he started believing he was seeing Mike
in London—in the turn of a cheek, a certain stride—he re-
gretted this. He thought maybe the problem could have been
avoided if he'd said good-bye with more finality, had seen
Mike's dead face. That seemed like part of the problem; it
was hard to accept that Mike was gone. He'd worked harder
than most for everything he'd attained. How could it be that
the one thing he couldn't work for was not granted to him in
large supply?

Ben thought the sightings might also be latent memories of the summer he'd spent with Mike in London. Three of
them had traveled on student visas between their junior and
senior years. Mike was the first to find a job: selling perfume
at Selfridges. Ben and Jason looked for work and went every
other day to the employment center, but, the fact was, Ben and
Jason didn't *have* to work. Their families could make up the
difference. Their families felt the experience of a summer in
London was more important than the money.

"Must be nice," Mike would say, counting out his food
budget for the week.

Mike hated selling perfume. He was working on com-
mission and his aggressive tactics didn't go over well with the
polished patrons of Selfridges. When he got a job at a pub in
Paddington, he switched immediately. And when the owner
offered him a chance to live in the flat over the pub, he moved
out the next day. Ben and Jason thought at the time it made
sense: the flat the three of them were sharing in Kensington
was tiny.

His frugality was extolled at the memorial service by
friends who'd known him longest. Newer friends spoke of his
generosity. His high school sweetheart remembered a camp-

ing trip during which Mike insisted they save as much money as they could on food; he was furious with her when she bought a name-brand pasta instead of a generic. Then an associate Mike worked with at the law firm spoke about the book club dinners Mike hosted, for which he usually prepared filet mignon. People shook their heads and wiped their eyes. It was like watching a beatification, a life of frugality rewarded with plenty, if only for a brief time.

His mother did not speak. Later, at their Italian dinner, Ben remembered her talking a lot, but at the service she sat silently in the front row, eyes glistening, feverish circles in her cheeks. Mike had always called her Maryanne, which allowed his friends in the years before they met her to picture an individual, not just a mother. And yet it also seemed to them a little unfeeling. Ben wondered what she made of some of the things said at the service. She seemed distracted, and rubbed her knees often. Several people spoke about what they gently phrased as Mike's difficult side—the temper and stubbornness that everyone who knew him encountered at one time or another and that could make people angry, desperate, even fearful when Mike was in a particularly perverse mood. At the memorial service it was variously described as having high standards for himself and his friends; as a fierce sense of loyalty; as perfectionism. All seemed true.

Back in London, Ben tried to shake off the mood. Each sighting had an explanation, after all. The shape of a face, the slope of a shoulder. These things were so strongly reminiscent of Mike that anyone would do a double take. He was sure of it.

He threw himself into work. When he could, he traveled. Never more than a three- or four-day weekend, typical of the life of the lawyer expat, particularly one in securities, but he thought it would help. He thought things would get better soon.

Looking around at the people in the booth with her, Maryanne understood it was time for her to order something to eat. She picked up the menu, sticky and smelling faintly of the cloth that must have been used to wipe it down after the last patron. She pictured a child, a little boy, hands covered with spaghetti sauce, then shook her head. Mike's friends had meant to be kind, bringing her here. She ordered his favorite, cheese tortellini, a silly thing to do, and when the tears filled her eyes she explained. The girl, Jenna, nodded.

"And he hated celery," said Ben, the boy with blue eyes and surprisingly long lashes.

Boys, girls. They were six years out of college, men and women now, Maryanne reminded herself.

Jenna ordered the tortellini, too. When Maryanne smiled at her, she shrugged and tucked her hair behind her ears. She was married to Jason, the quiet boy who was always slouching, though they were not wearing rings. So bold, these kids. Rings were a symbol they didn't need or didn't want; she couldn't remember how Mike had explained it to her.

"Should we have some wine?" Jason asked.

"Yes, certainly," Maryanne said.

"Red or white?"

"Red?"

They were having trouble hearing each other in the bright and bustling restaurant, but Maryanne smiled, suddenly grateful that they were here and trying. New York, an Indian summer. When they said they wanted to take her out to dinner after the memorial service, she requested somewhere casual.

"I didn't bring anything fancy," she told them. They chose Patsy's, downtown near NYU, but that meant nothing to her, so they brought her in a cab. The sign out front said the restaurant had been open since 1933. Did people really eat pizza then? she wondered. Someone must have, obviously, because here it was, with its small tables, yellow and green chairs, and tiny white floor tiles set in long crooked lines.

"Had you visited him?" she asked. "Had you seen his new place?"

The boys nodded. "Last New Year's Eve," Jenna said. "Right before Jason and I moved to Chicago."

"He was very proud of it," Maryanne said.

"Will Alex keep it?" Jenna asked.

The wine arrived, an uncorked bottle and four stubby glasses. While Ben poured, Jenna began a story about that New Year's Eve visit, something about hailing a taxi late on a freezing, snowy night. They walked for blocks and just when the rest of them gave up and resigned themselves to walking all the way back to Mike's apartment, "your son," Jenna said—and Maryanne's pulse quickened—"spotted a cab. He ran down the street, singing 'New York, New York,' waving his arms.

"We cut off two other groups of people," Jenna finished, smiling, wiping her eyes. "But Mike didn't care. He ushered us all in, then turned and bowed to everyone."

Maryanne pictured her son jumping into the car after such a performance, then she saw him jumping into their old station wagon, promoted to the front seat when he was ten.

She said, "You know, he never let me pay for anything when he was in college. I couldn't have afforded much, it's true, but I wasn't even allowed to buy him clothes I know he needed."

What had her point been? Thinking about Mike on a cold winter night, she guessed. Did he have a coat on? Was he warm enough? To the others she said, "I guess I was thinking about the dinner. I'd like to treat you all."

"Oh, no," said Jenna. "We invited you. It's on us."

Maryanne remembered a visit she'd made to Mike at Yale. They'd eaten in the dining hall because Mike had to work. She sat with his friends—these, she thought, and others—while he managed the salad bar. At the end of the meal, while the others talked and drank coffee, she watched him pull cellophane smooth and tight across the tops of large bowls.

"All right," Maryanne said.

The food arrived on heavy white plates. Sturdy plates, Maryanne thought, and wrapped her cold fingers around the thick edge. "Please go ahead," she said, "I'm going to let it cool."

They ate carefully, slowly. Jenna, in particular, held her fork sweetly. "You were all in the same residential college?" Maryanne asked. It had been years since that visit to Yale and she couldn't remember.

They nodded.

"And you boys were all roommates?"

Jason finished his bite quickly so he could answer. "Yes."

"And you two are married." Maryanne smiled at Jason and Jenna. "That's wonderful. Congratulations. I remember Mike telling me how much he enjoyed your wedding."

"Three years ago now," Jenna said.

"Any children?"

"Oh, not yet. But we'd like to."

She turned to Ben. "And what about you? Got a girlfriend on the horizon?"

He shook his head.

She seemed to be embarrassing them, so she picked up her

fork. Conversation flagged. Jenna seemed to want to tell more stories about Mike, but every time she started, she struggled to overcome tears. Maryanne wanted more wine, but would have liked one of the boys to pour it for her. Mike would have done that. She glanced around the restaurant. At the table where they were almost seated—before Jenna noticed Maryanne's expression and pointed to the more secluded booth—a family of five had just gotten their food. The mother was leaning over, cutting the pasta for her youngest child. In the far corner, their waitress was talking to someone in the kitchen, gesticulating, upset. The light in the restaurant had softened, and another waitress had started to light the small white candles on each table. It was the time of evening when it turned brighter inside than out.

"Well, that's wonderful," Maryanne said, stuffing energy into her voice with a big breath. "Girlfriends, new marriages. It's an exciting time for all of you."

Ben poured more wine for everyone.

Maryanne told them that she and Alex had chosen the flowers for the service that afternoon. Irises. She did not tell them that Alex had known this was Mike's favorite flower— had known he had a favorite flower. "I thought it was nice," she said.

The friends all agreed.

"I have a question," Maryanne said suddenly, brightly, and all three of them looked up. "I don't know how to get Mike's ashes home. On the plane. Will they make me put the box on the conveyor belt when I go through security?"

Jenna swallowed hard. Jason bowed his head. Ben, the lawyer, answered her. "I can look into that for you. I'm sure there's a better way."

They fell back into silence. Maryanne could think of

nothing else to say. The words she'd already said felt heavy, like sandbags against a dam. Why did she have to lead the conversation? Couldn't these kids, with all their education, do better? She folded her napkin in her lap.

The waitress appeared and asked if they needed anything else. Maryanne thought the woman had been crying, but no one else seemed to notice. "No, thank you," she said warmly, and the waitress smiled and left the check on the table.

Maryanne watched her thin back retreating. She could feel a headache beginning, but she didn't mind. She had a long night ahead packing up Mike's things with Alex and the headache would keep her quiet. She had a tendency to say too much; Mike used to tell her so.

"He had a crush on you," she said, turning to Jenna.

"Oh, no. I don't think so."

"Oh, just in the beginning, the first year of college. There was a girl he talked about a lot. Did you write for the newspaper?"

"Yes."

"Then it was you!"

"I don't know what to say." Jenna looked at Ben and Jason, but their faces were blank. "I see now," Jenna said, "I think we all do, how unhappy Mike was before he came out."

The boys nodded vigorously.

"I know," Maryanne said, and her tone surprised her. She patted her chest, twice, fast, as if to soften the hard edge they'd all heard.

Ben cleared his throat. He asked what she'd been doing the last couple of days.

So she told them about the pile of dirty clothes she'd found in Mike's closet. His debit card for the machines in his building still had twenty dollars on it. She pulled it out of her purse and showed them. It was attached to his key chain. "I always liked doing his laundry," she said.

The waitress came to clear the table and asked again if they wanted anything else. She stacked their plates on her arm, putting Maryanne's on top because it was still so full of food. "Wrap this up?" she asked.

"Yes, please," Maryanne said. "It was delicious." She would be embarrassed bringing another white Styrofoam box back to the apartment, but she was pleased to see the waitress smile.

Jenna, Jason, and Ben talked quietly of travel plans, where they were staying, when they had to be back at work. When they fell silent, Maryanne thanked them, as she had several times already, for coming so far so quickly, especially Ben.

"All the way from London. I just can't believe it. Do you enjoy living there?"

"It's only been a couple months, but yes. I do."

"Will you take a few days off now that you're home?"

"No, I can't. I have to get back."

"Mike loved it, too, I know. He used to talk about going back, after that summer when he had such a good time with you two. I never could interest him in Seattle."

The friends said they would stay in touch with her, and they wanted her to call if she needed anything. Jenna pulled a card out of her purse and wrote down all their addresses and phone numbers. She handed another, blank card to Maryanne. "Now give us your information," she said.

Maryanne smiled and wrote on her lap with an unsteady hand.

Soon the bill was paid and Jenna, Ben, and Jason made plans for the rest of the evening. Then Alex arrived, just as he said he would, perfectly on time. The tip was left in a jumble of bills and quarters, the waitress brought Maryanne her leftovers, and then they were out on the curb.

"Thank you so much," Maryanne said again. "I hope I'm not—"

Jenna stepped close and hugged her, stopping the words.

"I'll write to you," Jenna said. Then, while the boys were still talking, Jenna stepped into the street. A few minutes later, she held a yellow door open and Maryanne climbed in. Alex circled around and jumped in the other side. As the cab pulled away, Maryanne watched Jenna turn on Ben. She was mad at him about something and letting him know it.

"Did you have a good time?" Alex asked.

"Yes," Maryanne said, adjusting the white box on her lap.

The evening was warm and there was a gray wash over the city that made her eyes water. She rested her head on the back of the seat and pictured a snowy night, her son's cheeks red with cold. It was Jenna's voice she heard describing him, and she was grateful for the break from her own.

Ben drove west in a blue Ford Fiesta. He'd flown to New York on the red-eye after a frenzied week of packing. After two years in London, he was leaving his job. The firm didn't know yet. They thought they were transferring him back to the New York office and he was taking a three-week vacation while his belongings were in transit. But Ben had decided to rent a car and make the cross-country trek he had never managed in his youth, and at the end of it, he would make some changes, the first of which, in all likelihood, would be leaving the firm. He had a friend on the Hill who thought he could get him a job. He'd also been talking to Jason, who said the consulting firm he worked for might be able to do something. The important thing was that there were other possibilities and at thirty-one he had recognized them. It was September.

He drove fast, spending nights in cheap motels (he might as well be frugal, he thought, with so much up in the air), stopping for national parks and cities of interest. He was disappointed at how hard it was to get a beer after eight o'clock in the wide-open spaces of his country, but other than that he had few complaints. He drove until his back ached, then pulled into a motel and walked until the light faded and his feet hurt. At night he read until his vision blurred, books he'd never gotten to: *Great Expectations, The Grapes of Wrath.* He had one suitcase, a fine one from Bond Street, but that was all. He kept it in the trunk and carried it every night into the motel room, looking for all the world like a traveling salesman. It was not exactly backpacking across Europe, but he thought it shared a certain spirit and simplicity. He felt cheerful in a way he hadn't in years.

He intended to visit Mike's mother, Maryanne. She was on his mind when he mapped out a stop in Seattle, but crossing Montana he began to have doubts. Something about the straight, impossibly long roads. He had not talked to her since the trip to New York, and he wondered how she'd managed the last two years. He felt a brief glimmer of relief when he realized he probably didn't have her phone number, but when he next stopped for gas, he checked his address book and saw her name. He'd copied it there from the card Jenna thrust at him after that dinner.

"You were his roommate!" she'd said. "Stay in touch with his mother."

He'd kept the card on the refrigerator in London for months, and once, returning from the pub late, he'd almost called. But the intricacies of an international call were beyond him after five pints and he woke in the morning with the phone still in his lap.

He called Maryanne from a gas station an hour east of Seattle. He thought if he didn't get her he would still drive into the city and try again. Or maybe not. He would see how the day went. She answered, however, on the second ring. She was surprised but remembered him immediately. "Of course. How are you?" she said.

"I'm fine. How are you?"

"I'm fine. *Where* are you?"

He explained that he was near Seattle, driving across the country, and that if it wasn't too much trouble, he'd like to stop by and see her.

"Of course! You're very welcome. You can stay the night if you want."

He had not expected this. There was no reason not to spend the night, but instead he told her he was on a tight schedule, only a little time and a lot of people to visit. Just the afternoon would be best.

She gave him directions to her niece's house. She was living with her niece, she explained, helping with the children. He would meet them when he came. She sounded ebullient, something Ben had not remembered. He thought of Mike's mom as quiet and hardworking—she'd raised Mike alone after his father left. And something else: when Mike was a teenager, she challenged him to pull her hands off the steering wheel.

"A few times," Mike said. They were talking late one night in college. "On highways, sometimes. She wanted to see if I was strong enough."

"Had she been drinking?" Ben asked.

Mike looked at him. "No. She never drank."

"Did you ever do it?"

"Once. It didn't end well, but we weren't hurt. I remember her knuckles would go white."

The niece's house, outside Seattle, was a small, two-story clapboard with a front porch and dark green shutters in need of paint. The land was open all around, the nearest neighbor probably a quarter of a mile away, but a small backyard was nevertheless circumscribed by a chain-link fence. Two penned dogs, black and brown, barked as he pulled up. Toys, bikes, and parts of a jungle gym were scattered around, their plastic pinks and yellows dirty-bright in the green landscape. Maryanne stepped out when Ben was still on the porch stairs. The screen door stuck open behind her and she stopped abruptly. "Oh." She put a hand to her chest. "It's good to see you."

They were standing a few feet apart. Ben didn't know what to do. He'd never known her well. After the service in New York, he thought he would get to know her, help her. He'd had a sense of the role he could play and was not sure what to feel about the fact that he hadn't played it.

"Oh, come here," Maryanne said, and gave him a quick hug. Her hairstyle was out of fashion, but she was still lean and her face was smooth and healthy.

"It's good to see you," he said.

"Come inside. I've made a little lunch."

The house was sparsely furnished, a sofa and two chairs slipcovered in beige. Framed posters decorated the walls and the floor was carpeted wall to wall. When he hesitated in front of a picture of Mike, Maryanne picked it up and handed it to him.

"I have others I've been meaning to frame." She opened a drawer and took out an envelope full of photographs. She thumbed through them until she found a picture of a young

Mike, maybe nine or ten, standing under a tree. He was holding a giant chocolate cake, an enormous grin on his face.

"He won that at the school, in a cakewalk that was supposed to be for younger kids. Mike was so short he got in."
While she was speaking, Maryanne patted and stroked the
photograph. She touched Mike's face, the cake, Mike's sneakers. Then she abruptly stuffed it back into the envelope and
said, "This way."

Ben didn't know where to put the framed photo he was
holding, so he carried it with him into the small, bright kitchen,
where a wooden table was set for lunch: sandwiches and a bowl
of potato chips, homemade cookies and a pitcher of iced tea.
"There's also lemonade or beer, if you'd like," Maryanne said.

"This is great, but I wish you hadn't gone to so much
trouble."

"No trouble, especially since the kids are at school." Maryanne took the photo from Ben and set it on the table. "They'll
be back at three."

Ben nodded and asked for a beer.

Conversation was more difficult than he'd expected. They
spoke of the weather, long drives, the difficulty of repairing a
dishwasher. Ben complimented the kitchen, the sandwiches,
the potato chips—were they a local brand? He was wondering
whether he should mention Mike when Maryanne cleared her
throat. Are you still living in London? she asked. No, he just
moved back. What are you doing now? Well, he wasn't sure.
He was trying to figure that out. He told her he was hoping
the cross-country drive would clear his mind about a lot of
things.

"I see," Maryanne said.

Ben asked about her niece. She would be Mike's cousin?
Yes. How was she? Well, history was repeating itself: her hus-

band had left, but she had a good job at a bank. And the children? Amy and Lucy, seven and five.

The dogs barked suddenly and Ben used the distraction to glance at his watch. Only forty-five minutes had passed. Maryanne fixed him another half sandwich.

"That dinner in New York," she said. "A pizza place, wasn't it?"

As she recalled details, Ben grew uncomfortable. Maryanne remembered the dinner far better than Ben, even the name of the place, Patsy's. He remembered that they hadn't thought to take her to dinner at all, but couldn't say no to Alex, who needed a break from her presence in the apartment. Then they intended a different place, but couldn't get reservations, and Patsy's had been little more than a diner. The grieving mother had had to slide into a greasy booth. Jenna was distraught about it for weeks.

"I'm sorry I haven't stayed in touch," Ben said.

"How are Jenna and Jason?" Maryanne asked.

"Good, good. They're having a baby. In December."

"Oh, that's wonderful! I'll have to write her. She wrote me a letter, you know." Maryanne glanced at the photo of Mike, then stood up. "I'll show you, just a minute."

When she returned she was holding a card with a bouquet of daisies on the front. It arrived a few months after the memorial service, she said. She scanned quickly, then began to read.

"It was six o'clock in the morning and the sun was just beginning to rise, turning the sky a pale peach along the horizon. The city's night lights were still on, making the time of day seem ambiguous and unreal. In that weird half morning, on my way to New York for Mike's service, the bus passed what must have been a convent of some sort. I'd never noticed it before. As we passed I had a brief but very clear view of a plain room with white bare walls lit by candlelight. In the room, kneeling and motionless, were six nuns. I don't know if it was a trick of the strange light or because the faces were surrounded by white habits, but the immediate, striking impression I had was of small dark centers surrounded by folds of white, almost like flowers. I thought of Mike and our sad errand to New York and I looked at those nuns and knew they were praying for him. I believed so strongly, Mrs. Leary, that it brought tears to my eyes and I don't cry often. I know Mike would have had no use for such sentimental thoughts, but it made me feel better and I wanted to share it with you."

Maryanne put the letter down and blew her nose.

"Jenna's not religious," Ben said, more to himself than Maryanne.

She nodded, and Ben understood she believed he was mistaken or misinformed. She poured out some more potato chips and offered him another beer, which he accepted. While he drank and ate, she talked of the girls, her grandnieces. It was easier to get them the things they wanted now with the money Mike had left her, she said. She spent it all on them because she didn't feel right using any of it herself. She had everything she needed living with her niece and watching these children grow.

Ben left before any of the family came home. He told Maryanne he had only a couple of days to drive down the coast and all the way back to New York, which wasn't true. She seemed disappointed but did not question him. There was a brief moment when they might have made promises to keep in touch, but then they both smiled and Maryanne said, "Good luck, Ben. I hope you sort things out," and shook his hand.

"Mrs. Leary," Ben began, knowing he ought to do better.

"I always thought Mike was good, a really good person, and he was a great friend. I'm so sorry he didn't live longer."

"It's all right, Ben," she said.

He should have left then, but he decided to step in and give her a hug, something to make up for the inadequate words. As his right foot came down on her left, they both tottered. She patted his back. "I haven't really known what to do," Ben said.

"I know," said Maryanne and gently pushed him away.

The dogs barked as the car backed out of the driveway. Maryanne stayed on the porch, and Ben thrust his arm out the window and waved above the roof.

He drove into Seattle although he'd lost his enthusiasm for sightseeing. He stopped at a local coffee shop—the beers had made him sleepy—and picked up a frequent-customer card by the cash register. He held it a moment, staring at the little row of coffee mugs on grainy recycled paper, then touched the mugs the way Maryanne had touched the picture of Mike. Almost pawing. He stepped awkwardly out of the way of the next customer. He thought he might send the card to Jenna with a note about his visit with Mike's mom. Then he realized he would be doing that for all the wrong reasons, highlighting his role as the prodigal friend, not the misery of the broken mother, and he put the card back on the counter.

She had thought Ben was Mike for a minute as he came up the stairs. It had taken her breath away, and even now, hours later, the girls home and playing in the yard, she still felt the impact of that moment in the muscles of her body, everywhere, as if she'd been hit by a car.

Boys at certain stages all look alike. In college with all

that hair. Later, with foreheads, when their hairlines begin to recede. Maybe what had happened was that Ben looked a little bit the way Mike would have looked if he were still alive, coming to visit her, as he often did. They might have gone dancing, the way they did the time he came home to tell her he'd decided to go to law school. She was astonished at the invitation. She worried over her outfit and was ultimately disappointed in her choice, a dress, when she saw that the other women at the bar were wearing skirts or nice slacks. But it hadn't mattered. Mike knew she loved to dance.

She remembered Ben, thought of him driving away in his rental car, and smashed the kettle down on the burner. She pressed hard on the handle, imagining she had the strength to push it all the way through the stovetop and down into the oven below. When she released it, she exhaled loudly. She did not need this visit. A year ago, yes, but not now. She suspected it had helped Ben in some way—he didn't look well, had gained a considerable amount of weight.

"You can't come here now. You can't make this your story," she said loudly. She lifted and smashed the kettle on the stove once more, then clicked on the burner.

That service in New York? The firm's idea. To help her, they said, but she had just wanted to take her son home, away from the city that had changed him. The irises? Such a strange, furry-throated flower. In the confusion of the time she hadn't been able to remember that Mike also loved the phlox that grew by the side of their house. Could she have found phlox in New York? She would have tried if she'd remembered. There'd been the sound of traffic like a generator outside the windows. Her scratchy nylons. The things people said, sometimes with an apologetic glance. What? Did they think she didn't know her son? Of course he could be difficult.

She had not known Alex well, and, in truth, did not feel entirely comfortable around him then, but he was the only one whose words had made any sense to her and she'd thought a lot about that in the time since. "Damn the ocean, Mike! Damn the ocean," he'd said. The only one to mention the water! The water. She had not thought she had to keep her son safe from the water. After the service, the people who had been on Fire Island with Mike wanted to talk to her, but she did not want to be around those boys who had gone into the sea and come safely out again.

Lucy ran into the kitchen. She was five, full of herself. "When's dinner?" She dropped the ball she was carrying to open the refrigerator. It rolled beneath Maryanne's feet, nearly tripping her.

"I've told you not to bring your toys in here!"

The girl retreated and Maryanne sat down at the kitchen table and covered her eyes.

The pasta dinner in that awful restaurant. The apartment. The smell of Alex's coffee, worrisomely strong as she lay on Mike's bed, breathing into his pillow as slowly and deeply as she could, her anger mounting as she slowly lost his scent. The misery of learning she did not have to have him cremated. She could have afforded, with the money he left her, to bring his body home.

Maryanne slapped the table with her hand. What was Ben thinking, showing up now? She had thought he would be a friend, stay in touch. She hated to remember how she'd even thought he might become a second son. But only Jenna had written, the only bright spot in that dark time. She'd kept the letter in her purse for months, a live and humming thing that made her believe Mike still had a presence in the world.

She looked out the window at the girls. It's a fine life, she told herself. Stand up. Finish dinner. But she reached for Mike's picture and sipped her tea.

She didn't yell at the girls often—at least, she tried not to—but outside Lucy was warning Amy. She could tell by the way they were whispering, huddled together against the white sky. They needed new coats. She'd get them those shiny pink ones they wanted at the mall, with the real fur around the hoods. Matching scarves, hats, and mittens. Tomorrow.

She almost beckoned them inside, but didn't trust herself to stand. Maybe in a few minutes. Or maybe she would just let them play outside until dark.

NIGHT CLASS

Surprisingly skilled at grammar, and in possession of small, neat handwriting, Maryanne took a job teaching copyediting. The classroom was grubby, and the adult education students arrived tired and disheveled from the day jobs they were presumably trying to augment or leave, but the work suited her. She liked the chance to revise and perfect. It didn't feel like real life at all.

Over time she developed a little repertoire for acting out some of the marks in class. She bounced on her toes for the exclamation point. Her question mark was a subtle, full-body undulation. For brackets, she made an arc with her arms, then leaned over with impressive flexibility from the waist. This illustrated nicely, she thought, the effect of putting your upper body into a different clause from the one the rest of your soul was in.

Every semester at least one student, a little smug, asked if she'd wanted to be a dancer.

Oh, of course she had.

EVIDENCE OF OLD REPAIRS

Their first morning in London, a Monday, Sarah looked out the window and saw a squirrel eating from a woman's hand. Their hotel, the Royal Lancaster, stood on the north edge of Hyde Park. It was the middle of February, off-season, the only way they could afford to come, and the reason, Sarah believed, that they'd been given a room on such a high floor with windows facing south. These rooms went for much more in the summer, she was sure. They had a beautiful view over the Italian fountains at the top of the Serpentine and the park stretching away to the left and right. The landscape looked as though it had been drawn overnight in wet ink, the grass a moist dark green, the bare trees blackened by rain. Even the woman kneeling down to the squirrel was wearing a slick yellow raincoat that looked shiny and fresh.

Sarah shook her head in wonder. They had never had a room with such a view. In her life, she had rarely felt taller than the trees.

She called to her daughter. She thought Amelia would like to see that the squirrels were so tame.

Amelia, already up and dressed and reading at the table in the corner of the room, did not look up. "I'm reading," she said.

Sarah let the curtain fall closed and watched her. She was thirteen and pretty in a girlish way, not like some of her friends who already looked grown-up. She played the violin, seriously and well, and had an enviable sense of confidence. She was beginning to enter state competitions, and Sarah, sick with nerves in the audience, marveled at the self-possession she exhibited when she walked onto the stage. Other times, though, when Sarah watched her unaware, walking up the block from school or standing in the driveway waiting for a friend, this same calm manifested itself in a stillness, a quiet wariness that worried her.

"Any time you guys are ready," Amelia said, turning a page.

It was ten o'clock and her father was in the shower and Sarah was still in her robe. They'd said on the plane that they would try to get an early start each morning; they only had one week. But Sarah and Mark had been exhausted when the wake-up call came at eight. Amelia, however, had jumped out of bed. It was her spring break and her first time abroad.

"There are some squirrels eating out of a woman's hand in the park." Sarah turned back to the window and pulled the curtains wide open. This, as she had hoped, Amelia could not resist. She had always loved animals and that seemed not to have changed. She put down her book and came over.

"Down there." Sarah pointed. "On the left side of the water, past the fountains. See?"

Amelia nodded. "They're coming right to her hand. I wonder what she's feeding them."

"We could try it later. Would you like that?"

"Sure."

Sarah tried to see her expression, but Amelia kept her face turned to the park. What Sarah tried to remember is whether Amelia had had this stillness before. She'd been a good baby, never too fussy, and as a young child could play happily by herself for hours. From the day she entered school she'd been an excellent student, apparently motivated by an inner need to achieve. Still, Sarah was sometimes sure that there had been a spark in her eye, an easier laughter, that was now gone.

Mark came out of the bathroom. He was dressed and combing his hair. "All yours," he said to Sarah. Then, quietly, as she walked past him, "How are you?"

He was referring, she knew, to the fact that she'd had a drink on the plane. "Fine," she answered, trying to warm the coldness out of her voice. She was scared of flying, and anyway it had been almost four months since she had last had too much. "And you? How did you sleep?"

"Like a log," he said, kissing her on the cheek.

Sarah and Mark had come through a bad time after she discovered his affair, a year of silent dinners and midnight arguments. The affair was already over when she learned of it, and Mark had been the one to end it—of that she was certain. He swore it had been a mistake; that he was still in love with her. He was as committed as ever to the marriage, he said, and this did seem to be true. He proposed therapy, a suggestion that surprised her because he was such a private man, and a few months later the sessions seemed to come to a natural, satisfactory conclusion.

The counselor, beaming at them on the day of their final meeting, told them they were a great success. "Go into the world and love each other," he said, opening his arms wide as they left his office. The gesture made Sarah feel they should have been a pair of white doves flying out of a bag. She very nearly flapped her arms, but Mark took her elbow and guided her out of the building. It was spring and everything seemed back on track. They took down the storm windows and put up the screens. The daffodil bulbs she'd planted by the garage sent up clusters of green shoots. Then one evening—making julienne salad for dinner and waiting for Amelia to come home from her violin lesson and Mark to come home from the office—Sarah poured a shot of rum into her Pepsi. This in itself was not unusual, but tonight, sipping the cocktail, slicing the ham and cheese for the salad, the rum seemed to loosen the hold she had on herself. She poured another. Her mother had been an alcoholic, her grandmother one as well. Did this explain Sarah's problems? Sarah didn't think so, despite all the rhetoric of the age. She poured another drink. Two hours later the salad was a soggy confetti instead of the elegant strips it was meant to be and Sarah, looking deep into the white plastic bowl, knew this was a metaphor for her. She was in tears when Amelia and Mark came home, but on that night and the ones that followed, she was easily able to conceal what was happening. The fact of the matter was, she didn't drink that much. She never stumbled or slurred. She never got angry or abusive. And she never stopped doing any of the things they expected of her—laundry, shopping, cooking, cleaning. She just drank and got sad.

In the lobby, Sarah asked about the squirrels. Was feeding allowed? The concierge, kind but distant, with a smile that suggested pity rather than camaraderie, said that it was not recommended but it was not illegal; it was, in fact, quite a popular activity with the tourists, feeding the squirrels in Hyde Park. He went on to say that this time of year they could also see bunnies, geese, coots, moorhens, and magpies. It was too late for the mandarin duck and too early for the cygnets, two more favorites with the tourists. He held out a list of wildlife commonly spotted in London's parks, which Amelia took. The concierge bowed.

"Was he making fun of us?" Amelia asked Sarah when they were out on the street.

"Oh, it doesn't matter," she said. "We'll try it tomorrow, yes?"

Amelia nodded, and Sarah squeezed her arm. It was all she could do not to pull her into a full hug.

Probably no one ever would have found out. Sarah would have pulled herself together eventually, would have regained the control she felt she had almost intentionally surrendered. She was already having an easier time getting up in the morning and taking walks in the afternoon for exercise. But one day Amelia came home early from school and took a sip of Sarah's Pepsi. It was sitting on the counter by the kitchen sink, in the tall water glass Sarah always used.

"Mom?" she called.

Sarah had gone to the front door to get the mail. She'd only left the kitchen for a minute, but Amelia had used the side door. She must have been thirsty; her violin case was still slung over her shoulder.

"What's in this?"

"I'm having a cocktail," Sarah answered calmly. It was three o'clock in the afternoon.

"I don't believe this." Amelia looked at the floor, then quickly up again. "This is why you never share your drinks with me."

Sarah thought hard, but there didn't seem to be anything to say. It was true. She watched Amelia, who stood quietly watching her, seemingly replaying the previous weeks in light of this new information, questioning and judging everything that had been slightly out of the ordinary or difficult to understand. Coming to the end, to the ill-fated sip, she said again, "I don't believe this," and ran upstairs to her room.

Sarah imagined that ever after soda would be for Amelia what madeleines were for Proust, opening up whole chapters of memory, most of them painful. And the irony of it all was the timing. A few years earlier, her little pigtailed Amelia would have simply spat the mouthful into the sink and told her mother the soda had gone bad. A few years later, she might have smiled conspiratorially and asked if she could have one, too. But, at thirteen, Amelia was being subjected to a series of anti-drug classes at school that left her believing mood-altering substances of any kind slicked the road to hell. Sarah and Mark had always enjoyed a glass of wine with dinner. Now, this was nearly impossible. They sipped desultorily while Amelia harangued them with her latest facts and figures. "Did you know," she said one evening, "that an alcoholic can be defined as anyone who uses alcohol habitually?" From her chair at the side of the table, she turned left and right, raising an eyebrow at each of them, opposing players in the tennis match of her life. "What I see here, a glass of wine every night, is a habit."

And on this particular night, Amelia turned to her father before her first bite. Mark raised his wineglass in a mock toast to the evening lecture he believed was about to begin. Sarah, breathing slowly, stared at the store-bought peonies in the center of the table. It was odd how, even at this moment, she was proud of the arrangement she'd made.

"Something's wrong," Amelia said, her voice surprisingly timid.

They stood together on the north bank of the Serpentine; more accurately, Sarah now knew from studying the map at Lancaster Gate, the Long Water. She had pointed this out to Amelia and Mark.

"Long Water?" Mark said.

Tracing the map with her finger, Sarah started to say how the water was, in fact, if you looked at it, a long narrow shape before widening into the more irregular Serpentine, but Amelia interrupted her.

"Sort of long, maybe," she said, looking at her father to see if he would think this funny.

"Good point," he said, smiling.

Pigeons and seagulls were gathering noisily around their feet, but the squirrels Amelia was coaxing with the bread crumbs remained at a distance, scurrying about under cover of the wild bank beyond the iron fence that edged the path. It was nine o'clock, and the park was filled with slow runners and determined walkers. A few men and women in dark suits hurried by with briefcases and portfolios, their heels rhythmically crunching the brown pebbled path, their long coats flapping open as they walked. The air was cool, but the day was clear and the sunshine offered a bit of meager warmth.

Mark had been surprised by the proposal to do this first thing. He was ready with the guidebook, ready to see the

British Museum before lunch, the National Gallery after. But Sarah had insisted. "It won't take long, Mark," she said. "Just a half hour or so. Then we'll go to the museums." He appealed to Amelia, but when she agreed with Sarah, he conceded. Now he stood a few steps away, just a bit up the incline where the path curved gently to the left, his hands stuffed into the pockets of his coat. Sarah knew he didn't want to be here, but she also knew that he was wary of her, uncertain and therefore less critical. Amelia crouched low on the path, ticking and clucking with her tongue, and Sarah stood right behind her, more bread in her hand at the ready.

Planting daffodils by the garage had turned out to be a bad idea. It rained a lot that spring and the rain turned the bed to mud, which splattered up onto the white wall of the garage, and onto the long green daffodil leaves, and finally onto the lemon-yellow flowers themselves.

There were arguments, at night usually, and music during the afternoons. Rachmaninoff, Chopin, the "Humming Chorus" from *Madama Butterfly* (oh, it was the wakeful night of her soul, too), Lalo's *Symphonie Espagnole*. Sarah played them endlessly.

And Amelia, hearing the music, went straight to her room after school. Often, Sarah didn't see her until dinnertime, when Mark came home.

She stood by the kitchen window, making dinner and thinking about Amelia above. She wondered if Amelia was trying to concentrate on her homework while listening for the cabinet at the end of the counter opening, the splash of liquid meeting liquid. Probably she was. Sarah thought about going out and trying to wipe off the muddy daffodils, but cleaning a flower seemed like a strange and futile thing to do.

Each morning before sightseeing, Sarah and Amelia went to the east bank of the Long Water, where they faced Peter Pan, the sprightly statue in the clearing across the water. A straight line of mossy wooden moorings ran between the two banks, occupied, usually, by brilliant white seagulls, one to each pillar, while others soared overhead, vying for position. Occasionally a few shiny black cormorants moved in and easily commandeered a few spots on the row. It was a beautiful, chaotic scene that suggested to Sarah much larger bodies of water than a small lake in a park.

Remarkably, the seagulls, pigeons, and wood doves began to recognize their little family by the third morning and gathered quickly for their morning crumbs. This was noisy and exciting, and for the first time Sarah understood why children and the elderly love feeding the birds in parks. It was thrilling being the center of so much fluttering attention. For the squirrels, she collected rolls and crackers from their lunches. She ripped and broke these into small pieces and kept them in a plastic bag in her purse. The squirrels, however, would not take the food unless they put it on the ground.

"Mom, I don't think this is working," Amelia said the third morning. She stood up and looked doubtfully at her mother.

Sarah was kneeling on the path, her arm extended through the fence up to the shoulder. "Don't worry," she answered, slightly breathless with the effort.

Amelia brushed off her pants and crouched again.

Sarah tried to think of everything she knew about squirrels. She'd visited Assateague once, a barrier island off the coast of Maryland and Virginia. The gray squirrel was endangered there and was being reintroduced. Boxes had been nailed to trees all over the island for them to nest in. At night, to check their population, park rangers went around with dim flashlights, lifting the roofs of the boxes and counting the sleeping squirrels inside. Each family had to be accounted for.

But what did squirrels eat?

"You don't have to try so hard," Amelia said.

"Yes, we do," Sarah said.

It was Wednesday and Mark had brought a cup of coffee to the park. He was sitting on a bench nearby, hunched forward, sipping. He was watching them, his face pale and blank.

"Peanuts," Sarah said suddenly. "Amelia, tomorrow let's try peanuts."

By the time the chrysanthemums in the side bed were in bloom (during a cold dry autumn that made the reds and oranges as vivid as Sarah had ever seen them), she understood Mark and Amelia's fears better than she did her own behavior, so it made sense to seek help. She went to AA, but after three weeks felt certain that her problem was not that of the classic alcoholic. She didn't fit the profile. Once before in her marriage she had had a bout of drinking, but after a few months stopped. Wasn't a real alcoholic permanently recovering, never allowed to have another drink? But she had gone back without a problem to having a glass of wine with dinner and even a cocktail or two at parties. AA referred her to ACA, Adult Children of Alcoholics, but this didn't help either. Same prayers, more blame, it seemed, and she didn't want to blame her mother; none of it felt like her fault. Once, when she was twenty-five or so and had finally as-sembled a few facts about her family, Sarah asked her mother, Margaret, why she'd never talked about the difficulties of her own childhood, her ordeals with her mother.

But Margaret just stared at her. "And when should I have told you about it?" she said. "Over which peanut-butter-and-jelly sandwich?"

She had always thought her mother's point a good one. It reminded her of something else she'd liked to say, "Let the problems of the day be sufficient unto the day." The same should be true for generations, her mother felt, and Sarah agreed. She gave up all acronyms and vowed to quit drinking again on her own. It was mid-October and, except for one night in November, she did.

Passing through the lobby on their fourth morning, Sarah noticed that the concierge smiled and gave a little salute in Amelia's direction. She turned quickly to see Amelia grin and wave back.

"Did you speak to him again?" she asked when they were outside. Somehow it felt like a betrayal.

"I asked him where to get peanuts," she said.

In the park, several aggressive geese joined the melee, as well as a few mallard pairs with impeccable manners. Quiet and noble, they took what was within reach and left the fren-zied hunting and pecking to others. The number of birds seemed to be a deterrent to the squirrels, so Sarah sent Amelia farther down the path to try to lure the squirrels from the underbrush while she fed the birds in the clearing.

Mark, this morning, had brought a newspaper with his coffee. Amelia asked him if he wanted to help.

"Oh, I don't think so," he said, smiling at her. "This is your and your mother's thing."

Sarah demurred from where she was standing a few steps away. "Come on, Mark," she said. "We're just feeding the animals here. You're welcome to join in." She sounded annoyed. She tried to lob a piece of bread gently in the direction of a retiring female duck, but it hit her on the head.

Mark turned to Amelia. "I don't think so," he said again and began to unfurl his newspaper.

"Right," Amelia said. "I understand."

Perhaps it was because the yard hadn't been raked all season. Or maybe it was because Sarah woke flushed and irritable after a late nap on a gray November afternoon. Whatever the reason, when she went outside to get some air, to try to cheer up, she began surveying the back of the house, the yard, the neighboring houses, the other backyards. Little rectangular plots of land abutting the vulnerable backs of houses. Windy screened-in porches, peeling paint, thick black wires like spindly buttresses connecting everyone to the central nave of telephone poles running down the center of the block. Their own yard needed tending to, the garage painting. There was a honeysuckle bush that had been allowed to grow into a sort of tree with a trunk so off-center and twisted it had to be supported with a two-by-four. There was a hackberry by the side patio that was so storm-ravaged Sarah counted seven blunt branches where the tree had once stretched out into a lovely shape. It brought tears to her eyes, rising, as it did, in its broken, awkward way above their house.

The sky was pale blue, fading nearly to white in the east, and the sunset was obscured by a low, cluttered horizon of trees and houses. Music, an upbeat march punctuated by steady percussion, drifted to her from the direction of the stadium: the university marching band practicing for the game that weekend. The town suddenly seemed very small, crosshatched and cinched together by nothing more than telephone cables and marching bands.

That was when she decided to plan the trip to England. But she also decided, heading down the driveway toward the kitchen door, that she would have a drink to warm herself and rake the yard.

They were amazing, they really were. Sometimes Mark and Amelia heard a high pitch that no one else could hear; sometimes their eardrums, more sensitive than most, were disturbed by a vibration that no one else could feel. They would look at each other quickly, checking to see if the other one felt it, too. Then they would plug their ears or rub them, shaking their heads together in smiling bewilderment.

When this happened in the restaurant in Piccadilly where they were having lunch on their fifth afternoon, Sarah put down her soup spoon and looked back and forth between them. "You are just two peas in a pod," she said.

"Mom, stop," said Amelia.

"What? It's true," she said. "You're very like your father, Amelia."

"Mom, we both have sensitive ears. It's no big deal."

"Oh, I think it is."

An argument might have started if it weren't for the music that came on in the restaurant just then. They all recognized it: Rachmaninoff's Second Piano Concerto, one of Sarah's favorites, only in a terrible Hooked-on-Classics version with a steady beat in the background. It was like a parody of their family grief, the comic score in place of the tragic. It was so reminiscent for all of them of the dark months of Sarah's drinking that none of them knew what to say or where to look. This was not the first time music had united them in this way, engulfing them suddenly like an afternoon squall. And as on those other occasions, Sarah thought how this feeling, this mutual discomfort, was like a dark figure whom she had brought into their midst and now couldn't dismiss. She was astonished by the injustice. She had not done what Mark had done. She did not have his career or Amelia's talent. What she had was them, her family. How could she be the one who had caused the most damage?

It was drizzling when they left the restaurant. Mark stepped forward and opened one of their two umbrellas. Amelia started after him, but then stopped and turned. Someone watching might have missed the moment of indecision. She stepped quickly back up the curb and joined her mother under the second umbrella. It was an apology, Sarah knew, not her wish, but she took it, squeezing Amelia's hand.

Raking leaves. Because it was something Mark usually did, it had not occurred to Sarah that the job would include clearing the leaves out of the evergreen bushes that lined the front of the house. Dry yellow and brown leaves littered the top of the bushes, and some had nestled down into the dense dark green needles for the season. She worked with her hands until they were scratched and raw, then switched to the rake. It was a strange and wonderful thing, beating those bushes with the rake.

The morning of their last full day was still and white. A low mist the color of the sky skirted the trees in the park. It was warmer than it had been all week and smells from blocks away—fish, burning coffee, diesel fumes—hung in the air in pockets. The surface of the water was glassy, the wake of a single coot rippling in long lines undisturbed. Walking past the Italian fountains, which were not yet running, Sarah felt that sounds, too, were attenuated. Somewhere in the distance she heard the noise of construction, and she walked carefully, listening to her shoes on the path.

The day before, the squirrels had finally taken a few peanuts from their hands, hers and Amelia's. It had delighted them both and relieved Sarah, as she felt this was something Amelia would certainly take home with her, something she would always remember about their trip to London. It was worth the time spent, Sarah knew, because Amelia loved animals and would tell all her friends how they'd gone to the Serpentine every morning, persevering until they'd earned the squirrels' trust. It was something they had succeeded in together, and she thought it would grow, over time, into a good memory for Amelia, an example of her mother at her best.

They were back early this morning because Mark wanted to memorialize the event in pictures, a suggestion Sarah appreciated. The squirrels came to their fingertips again, and although it was impossible to tell, she thought they must be the same ones.

"Why don't we name them?" she said to Amelia.

"Name them?"

"Well, after this week, don't you feel like you know them?"

"After this week—" Amelia started, but she stopped and shook her head.

Sarah said cheerfully, "Well, I do. What about George and Lucy? And the one in front of you could be Camilla. Or maybe that's too fancy for a squirrel?"

Amelia remained quiet, avoiding her mother's gaze. A few minutes passed, and Sarah said softly, "I was trying to be funny."

Amelia nodded.

When they had only a handful of peanuts left, Mark came over and said he wanted to give it a try.

Sarah stood. "Why?"

Mark stared at her. "Oh, look. The thing's done. I just want to see if they'll come to me, too. We leave tomorrow."

Amelia, still on the ground, made a stream of kissing noises to soothe the squirrels.

Mark reached for the bag of peanuts Sarah held. When she did not offer it to him, he stuck his hand in awkwardly and took a few. Then he leaned over from the waist, the camera bag swinging forward suddenly. The squirrels scattered.

Sarah said, "It takes patience, Mark. You have to crouch down."

He crouched, and with Amelia clucking and ticking, the squirrels cautiously approached.

"Hold it out to them," Sarah said.

Mark extended his arm.

"It would be better if you put a few on the ground first, until they're used to you."

Amelia looked up. "Mom," she said.

Sarah turned and walked up the path to the clearing. Across the water, smoke rose behind Peter Pan, and the smell of burning leaves filled the air. With his arms up the way they were—as though conducting a fairy symphony—and the smoke behind him, it looked to Sarah like he was about to jump into the water. She concentrated on him and imagined his dive, just how it would look, how the water would splash up behind his tiny heels and the birds all around would rise and circle in the air, the seagulls' cries echoing over the park. After a while, they would settle down again, unperturbed by the empty pedestal.

When she looked back at Mark and Amelia, they were standing, deep in conversation. The squirrels were gone.

"So," she said, approaching. "I see you two have moved on to more important things."

Mark looked away and Amelia said, "Why are you being like this?"

Sarah was surprised at her answer. "Ask your father," she said and turned to walk alone down the path.

She was still in the front yard when Amelia came home. She was on her second rake, the first's handle having splintered. Even in her state, she recognized the agony on Amelia's face, her usual protective distance uprooted by fear and confusion.

Sarah stopped. She wanted to help her. "Amelia," she said. "It's okay."

"Right, Mom. That's great. Will you come inside now?"

"I'm just finishing here."

"Mom, you're done. What are you doing?" Her eyes were red, filling with tears. The bushes on either side of the front door were smashed in sections, holes where thick needles had been. Many of the smaller branches hung down, broken, showing splinters of pulpy white underbark. Trails of leaves ornamented the yard, some of them leading across the driveway and onto the neighbor's grass.

"Oh, sweetie," Sarah started. She took a step toward her, but Amelia took a step back. Sarah dropped the rake.

She leaned over to pick it up, reaching out to balance herself on the ground. "The leaves were, you know, stuck and—"

"Okay, please come inside, Mom. You can tell me there."

"Amelia, you're overreacting. If you'd just listen—"

"Listen? To what? You're hitting the bushes with a rake, the yard is a mess. Were you trying to rake the leaves into the gutter? Because if you were, Mom, you missed. The Mallons aren't going to be very happy."

"Don't worry about it, sweetie."

"Don't call me that! I hate it. No one calls me that except you."

"I'm sorry," Sarah answered. Now that she was no longer raking, she was cold. She didn't have on a coat. Amelia, perhaps sensing that danger was past, turned violently and went into the house. Sarah followed.

When Amelia ran upstairs, Sarah poured herself another drink. She sipped it standing by the kitchen sink and listened to Amelia getting ready to practice. She was upset, she knew, because it wasn't like her to practice first. She usually rested or did some homework. She started with scales and they were fierce and fast. Sarah had played the violin as a child so knew enough to marvel at her daughter's technical ability. She really was so good, Sarah thought. Suddenly she was sad and proud and filled with the desire to tell Amelia that her teacher had said she was good enough to have a concert career if she wanted to. Sarah headed up the stairs.

The door was closed but unlocked and Sarah opened it without knocking. Amelia ignored her. There was a wicker chair in the corner of the room, and Sarah aimed for it and sat down as quietly as she could. When the chair creaked loudly, she grinned. "Sorry," she whispered.

Amelia finished her scales and warm-up exercises and started thumbing through a book of music. It was clear she wanted Sarah to leave.

"Could I just stay a little bit longer? I really like to listen to you. You're so good."

Amelia looked at her. "Mom, don't do this."

"Do what?"

"Mom, stop."

"Sweet—" she clapped a hand over her mouth. "I don't understand," she said through her fingers.

Amelia glanced around her room as though searching for assistance, then looked down at her violin. "Will you just go away, please?"

"Why? I promise to be quiet. You won't even know I'm here."

"Oh, right. I can smell you."

This was new territory and it surprised them both. Generally they stayed away from the particulars. Amelia stared, waiting, Sarah knew, to see if she would be angry. But she wasn't. It was okay, she thought.

"Yes," she said, swallowing hard. "I know it. But can I tell you why I think I had a drink tonight?"

"No, it's okay," Amelia said quickly. Then they were both quiet and ashamed. The gray light through the blue curtains filled the room. Amelia moved slightly and turned on her music lamp. After a moment, she picked up her violin. She began a slow piece by Satie that Sarah had told Amelia she loved. It was not something new. It was a piece Amelia had already performed. This was a reprieve, Sarah knew, and started to cry, not for the music, but for the time when Amelia would no longer be willing to give her such gifts.

THE ESSENTIALS OF ACCELERATION

I am a good driver, and by this I don't just mean safe. Like a good runner who doesn't waste motion in her stride, I maneuver my car with dexterity and precision. I merge smoothly and without braking. In three moves, I can parallel park on either side of the street. One of my friends is the mechanic at the corner garage. He respects my studious approach to the art of driving and I admire his work. He's honest and his hours are reliable, unlike the dry cleaner up the street who repeatedly closes at ten to seven and will not open the door even if you point out the time. Leo, the mechanic, is Mexican. His family also owns Guadalajara across the street, where I occasionally have a burrito.

I am not married, and I haven't traveled as widely as my father, though I would like to. After college I drove across the country with a friend, but that was twenty years ago. I went to Copenhagen as a teenager because my mother wanted to see it at Christmas. Mexico intrigues me now that I'm friends with Leo. It would be interesting to see his home. And by *home*

I don't mean his home isn't America. I assure you I understand this, though my father does not.

Our neighbors assume that because I live in a house with my father we are a close family. I'm forty-one, he is ninety-one, and I am his only child. He built the house the year he was fifty, the year I was born, his only act of practical construction in an otherwise wholly intellectual life. He's an English professor at the university, emeritus now, though they humor him with a little closet of an office he still goes to on Wednesdays. While the house was under construction, my parents lived next door, in the small bungalow now owned by my neighbors, the Prestons. I much prefer that house, but my father built a two-story brick colonial for himself and his bride because that was a design generally admired when he was a newlywed and he wanted to build one. A writer and a teacher, he wanted to lay bricks. He wanted to work with his hands. It is the largest house on the block in a neighborhood that has too many rentals. Ours is not a gentrified area, not yet prettified and landscaped. One street over, for example, there's a handmade, laminated sign clothespinned to a piece of overgrown privet hedge telling drivers—and not politely—to avoid blocking the front walk. I love that sign.

My father lived in this house on Thomas Lane with my mother for twenty years, without her for twenty-one. Ten years ago he moved to the basement apartment, his choice, and I moved into the main house. My father still has excellent eyesight and a flawless record and he drives his own car. He's easily distracted, however—a cardinal in the snow, a patch of purple phlox by the roadside. But at the Department of Motor Vehicles last year they simply checked his vision, crowded his head with compliments about his age, and let him go. He is the oldest licensed citizen in Charlottesville. Every spring, right around his birthday, there's a little story about him in the paper with a picture.

Everyone knows my father. He leaves flowers—roses or peonies, typically—on our neighbors' doorsteps. For this he saves plastic gallon milk jugs to use as vases. It takes him an exceptionally long time to finish a gallon of milk, so to supplement his stock he pulls containers from the bins at the recycling center. Many have seen him; there's been a story in the paper about this, too. He cuts off the tops of the jugs, fills them with water, sticks in the flowers from his garden, and sets out, sloshing water everywhere, down his beige pants, onto his white shoes. I asked him once why he couldn't just use jars. Jars are easier, I pointed out. Smaller. And between the two of us we might generate enough so he wouldn't have to collect them from the recycling center. This was his answer:

"Holly, I'm sorry the Lord didn't give you a husband and children. But if He had, what you would know is folks on our street don't want a glass vase on the doorstep. A small child could knock it over, the glass would break, and the child might get hurt."

I try to be neighborly. I am quiet and neat. I don't keep wind chimes, for example, because some consider them noise pollution. I rake my leaves on time. I mulch around my trees and shrubs. I have never left the Christmas wreath up past the first of the year or a pumpkin out past Thanksgiving. I shovel my front sidewalk and throw down salt to melt the ice. I do not, however, wish to make friends with people just because my father roams the street with flowers. I don't wish to be treated as good and lucky simply because I have an older father. I know he keeps the neighbors—mostly women at home with their babies—talking for long periods of time. I know every conversation, no matter how it begins, finds its way back to

World War II or growing tomatoes. He must tire people with his stories about who used to live in their houses sixty years ago and the "Negro" part of town. Everyone seems interested at first, but how many times can you pretend to be impressed that Mrs. Profitt raised nine children in the two-bedroom bungalow you consider a starter home and plan to live in only until you have a second child and move across town to the bigger houses and better schools?

I suppose people like my father out of some sense that it is right to honor the past. No one says "Negro" anymore, but no one tries to grow a ripe tomato from seed by the fourth of July anymore, either. His age earns him the right to surprise people with his vocabulary and hobbies while their babies nap or idle in strollers or tear about the lawn. Like an old cat who drools, he is forgiven. He's ending his life on Thomas Lane; they're starting theirs. If they notice this framing, they think it poignant. But not for one second do they think they might end their lives here, too, in such modest surroundings, on such a narrow road, on the wrong side of the railroad tracks from the university.

I try to be a dutiful daughter. I take him to doctor appointments, buy his groceries, and occasionally pick up a new sweater or pair of trousers for him at the mall. My father is a nice old man, and by this I mean he is kind to his neighbors, tends his garden, reads a lot, tries to stay fit. He's a good Christian and tries to love those who are different from him. The problem is we don't have much in common.

When I left the house the other day, the woman across the street pulled out of her driveway behind me. She drives a Honda minivan as new as her latest pregnancy. She already has two children, one dog, and a cat, and I have sensed in her a grow-ing irritation. She's an ex-lawyer and her husband's a lawyer for the university. Before long they'll move to Rugby Road, I'm sure, but for the time being the babies seem to be coming faster than the promotions. Before we'd reached the stop sign at the end of the street, she was tailgating.

I turned right, and so did my neighbor. I glanced in the rearview mirror and saw from her posture that she was frus-trated with me. But what had I done other than drive carefully up a narrow street well populated by young children and pets, many of them hers? As we approached the first light, her right turn signal came on, so I clicked mine on, too. I guessed she was going to Barracks Road Shopping Center, a frequent destination of young mothers as it has both a twenty-four-hour grocery store and one of the most popular coffee shops in town.

We drove the length of Jefferson Park Avenue bumper to bumper. I held the wheel at ten and two and avoided looking in my rearview mirror. I turned a couple of times to admire the alternating pink and white dogwoods in the median. I do admire them, but nothing frustrates an impatient driver more than another driver enjoying the scenery.

At the end of Jefferson Park Avenue I kept left, anticipat-ing Barracks and the coffee shop, but she swung out to the right, toward the hospital, and merged fast, beating the on-coming traffic by a small margin.

I admit I was nervous for a few minutes. She wasn't yet to three months, a common window for miscarriage. But I learned later there was no emergency. She was merely on her way to the hospital to visit a friend who'd had a baby. I don't think she even knew it was me she was tailgating. The next day she waved pleasantly from her front porch.

Mothers like her are accidents waiting to happen, I tell you, and by that I mean they think they are the only drivers on the road. In England, I've read, you can take an advanced driving test for which you have to prove you are not just a competent driver, but supremely competent. It's not sufficient to master the laws of the road; you must demonstrate a higher level of awareness. One of the things tested, for example, is your ability to keep your speed constant on hills. Most drivers slow down on the ascent and accelerate on the descent, a hill-driving method that wastes gas, taxes the brakes, and annoys the drivers behind them. Is it so very hard to understand that more acceleration is needed to counteract the incline?

My mother insisted I learn to drive on a manual transmission. There was a class at my high school, half a semester of driving split with half a semester of health, but she disdained the idea of my learning to drive in school, and the school cars were automatic. So I took an art class and drove with her in the evenings that fall. Every night for a week we circled the block. When I could do this without stalling or making any mistakes, she let me go farther. We listened to the radio, oldie stations my father disliked. She would bring two cans of soda, though I wasn't allowed to open mine until the lesson was finished. I drove while she sipped happily, marking the rhythm of the songs with her hand on the door and a little bounce in her chin. "There's a lot of sky in Charlottesville," she said once. Another time toward the end of the semester we were heading past the university. She pointed at the Christmas-decorated balconies of the student dorms. "Little rectangles of cheer," she said. I was sixteen. She died when I was twenty.

Now when I tell Leo over my Monday burrito that my mother taught me to drive he says, "No."

"What do you mean, no?"

"It's a father's job."

"In all other ways my parents had very traditional roles. But my mother was a good driver."

Leo seemed amused. "Your father is not?"

I didn't know how to answer that question, so I just said again that it was my mother who taught me to drive.

There is a place in town, the light at the intersection of University and Main, where I can leave the car in gear, take my foot off the gas, and the car won't move forward or backward. It's absolutely flat. I pointed it out to my father recently. We were on the way to one of his doctor appointments. He was not driving himself because his car was in Leo's garage, and when we drive together, I'm always the driver. He seemed interested in my observation, which was gratifying, but then he said something odd. He sat quietly a moment, facing forward. Behind us someone's tires squealed.

"Never has a country so in love with the automobile driven it so poorly."

I braced myself. My father has a way of making the universal feel personal. "What do you mean, Dad?"

"We no longer really walk anywhere or sail." He cleared his throat, and I wondered if he'd been planning this speech. "The spirit of flying is dead, space exploration is a joke. Our affair with the car, however, continues. The names alone express all our hope for adventure and riches. Look at that."

We were behind an Expedition. In front of us one lane over was a Sable.

"And the Taurus?" I asked.

"What's that?"

"This car, a Ford Taurus. We're in a Taurus."

He looked at me. "Your car is a Taurus?"

"Yes. Just like yours, but I have the sedan. Didn't you know that?"

"I did not know that."

The light changed and I pressed the gas pedal indelicately. I knew what he was thinking, but did not want to give him the satisfaction of an argument. He thinks I'm stubborn.

A little while later he said, "'*Ask me for my biography and I will tell you the books I have read.*' Do you know who wrote that?"

I shook my head.

"Osip Mandelstam."

Frankly, I've lived long enough as a nonacademic in an academic town. I work in the office of the university landscaper, a job my father tolerated when I got it nearly twenty years ago because it's connected to the university, and he loves to garden. I'm still there, however, a manager more than a gardener, by which I mean I do not own a pair of gardening gloves. My mother loved books, my father is a professor, our house is full of bookshelves, but I am not a reader. I read more than the average American, according to the newspaper, but it's not for me an essential activity.

By the next light I had an idea. "Fiesta, Taurus, maybe next an Expedition. Do you know what those are?"

My father shook his head.

"The names of the cars I've owned."

I'm aware of sometimes being unkind. But he has said before I care too much for my cars, by which he means I should have had children. My usual reply is that if you have a child when you're fifty, as he did, there are some things you should not expect to see.

I have never asked him if he is disappointed he did not have a child more like him because I know the answer. Which is why it surprised me when he spoke again and said, "I think you needed a different kind of father."

I was so startled I almost forgot to check my blind spot before merging into the passing lane. The car I passed had its windshield wipers going even though it wasn't raining.

"In czarist Russia," my father said, "a lit candle in daylight was considered a harbinger of death. I have always felt a similar unease about the unnecessary use of windshield wipers."

And so the moment to respond was gone.

My pregnant neighbor stopped by yesterday. When I answered the door she asked for Mr. Levering. I told her my father answers his own door, the one on the north side of the house. She frowned, but turned and left the porch. A few minutes later, she knocked again.

"There's no answer."

I waited, wondering what she wanted me to do.

"Could you give him this?" She handed me a small pink envelope.

I started to say his door had a mail slot, but stopped. I'm aware of sometimes going too far.

"I notice his car's in the drive." She glanced up and down the street. "But I don't see him outside."

Leo told me he remembers American tourists coming to his town when he was a boy. They worried excessively about the roaming, homeless cats. They wanted to feed them, name them. What a luxury, his mother would say, to have time to worry about cats!

My neighbor is pregnant and has two other children under the age of three. She has an overgrown yard, a gas-guzzling car, and a workaholic husband, and she has time to worry about my father? Does this make her a better person? I suspect she shakes her head over dinner on the rare nights when her husband is home and says, "I don't understand Holly Levering. Why doesn't she look after her father better?"

She thinks she would.

I took the note from her and followed her down the front steps, then turned the corner of the house and aimed the note through my father's mail slot. When I stood up, I saw her watching me from the street. Thomas Lane doesn't have sidewalks. I smiled and waved.

If being a friend and being a neighbor are the same thing, why do we have two different words? A few of the neighbors are new, and by that I mean they've been here five to ten years. But a couple have lived on the street longer than that and not one of them has ever asked about my mother. Maybe they think she's living somewhere else? Tell me, when do you work into a conversation that your mother died in a car crash? Somewhere between bringing over the first pie or housewarming gift and the ninth or tenth Christmas without so much as an invitation for a holiday drink? Am I supposed to blurt out the information for their benefit, to explain my eccentricities? Maybe I should write it out on a laminated sheet and clip it to our front hedge? Yes! Let's have laminated sheets up and down the street announcing all our personal disasters and resentments. That would be helpful, perhaps even neighborly.

Leo says the formula for getting through the week in a small town in a small job is rhythm and routine, and I think he's onto something. My routine includes a burrito twice a week, once on Monday after work by myself, and again on Wednesday with my father after he gets home from his office at the university. Leo calls my father "the professor" and my father calls Leo nothing after I told him "the Mexican" was not appropriate.

"The chef?" my father asked.

"He's not, though. He's a mechanic. He's just a server here sometimes."

"Now who's judging," my father said.

There is absolutely nothing to recommend Guadalajara over any other Mexican restaurant in town except that I know and like Leo. It is small and has a view of a parking lot, though most places in Charlottesville do. It is also within walking distance of the house and it's nice to know I can occasionally enjoy a beer or two with my dinner and not have to worry about the drive home. My father always arrives separately.

"How are you, Professor?" Leo asks and puts in the order for the pork chalupas he likes.

"Fine, sir," my father answers with a small bow.

They feign a courtliness I don't understand. I asked Leo about it once and he just smiled.

I asked my father if he'd gotten the pregnant neighbor's letter.

"She has a name," he said. "Janeen."

"They all do, I presume. Do you think she knows mine?"

My father continued as if he hadn't heard me. "And the children are Annabelle and Henry."

We ate for a few minutes. For an old man, my father eats neatly, which is a blessing.

"What was it about?" I asked.

"The flowers."

The envelope was in his pocket, and he showed it to me: a thank-you note for one of his bouquets, scrawled by Annabelle. The food arrived, and I ordered a second beer. At the end of our meal, my father said he'd like to walk home.

"What about your car?" I asked.

"I'll get it tomorrow."

Sometimes I'm surprised we can talk about cars so casually.

"Dad, you won't want to walk up here tomorrow. I'll drive it for you."

"Sure I will."

But I drove it home for him and I shouldn't have because I'd had the two beers.

I am the neighbor you don't know. The neighbor who doesn't do anything wrong, but for some reason you just don't like her very much. Maybe it's the way she treats her elderly father. You think she could be nicer. You've lived down the street ten, fifteen years and know her no better than you did the day you moved in. You've asked her for favors: Bring in the mail while we're away? Water the garden? But she's never asked you for a favor in return. Maybe you have a smattering of memories, mostly visual: watching her haul her Christmas tree home, shovel her car out of the snow, drive a wreath of pink roses somewhere every spring. Is it every spring? No, more often than that, surely, but you can't quite remember.

Neighbor must be one of the most flexible words in the language. And by that I mean you can say "she's my neighbor" and people will think you mean she's your friend. But if something goes wrong, you can say, "Oh, I don't really know her. She's just my neighbor," and everyone still knows what you mean.

Janeen told the police she didn't think I had a drinking problem. "Then again," she said, "I don't really know her. She's just my neighbor."

A witness said the boy was never really all that close to the car.

In the paper it became "Daughter Transporting Mother's Roadside Memorial Has Traffic Accident," which is strange for two reasons. First, there was no "traffic." I missed the boy and hit the parked silver Lexus of the wealthy college student living in the house her parents bought her. I did this intentionally. It was either the Lexus or Mr. Braden's prize yellow butterfly bush and I like him better. No other cars were involved and the boy was unhurt. Second, I wasn't "transporting" the wreath. I didn't even know it was in the trunk. I was supposed to pick it up in the morning.

I *was* going too fast, however, that much is true. The two beers and a small dinner meant my judgment was impaired, no question, though my blood alcohol level was not over the legal limit. The officer was young and apologetic.

"I'm sorry," he said. "I have to ticket you, but I don't really think you're a threat."

I thanked him and thought it best to say nothing more. I wasn't sure he was right. Sometimes I think I know a few big things about me and my family more than I know one single true sentence.

You can't spend a lot of time driving, as I do, and not think about the dangers. The skill of driving defensively is seeing danger everywhere. Over the years an archive of accidents, a mental flip-book of tragedy, has stuck in my head. My mother, of course. The woman who was crossing the street in front of her church in Washington, hit so hard by a car her head was severed from her body and flew a hundred feet. The preschooler waiting in her car seat one morning while her aunt

dug out after a snowstorm. The aunt turned the car on to keep
the girl warm, but the exhaust pipe was in the snowbank and
she died of carbon monoxide poisoning before the driveway
was clear. Through the window, the aunt saw the little girl fall
asleep and thought she was just tired. The pastor who left his
baby in the car while he went in to work one day last summer.
He was supposed to take her to the day-care center but forgot. He found her late in the afternoon, dead from heat stroke.
What is that man supposed to do? Find God? He was already
a pastor. Who will he talk to now?

　　The local school crossing guard tells me she is not allowed to touch anyone crossing the street, not even the little
old ladies who stand on the curb and flutter their elbows like
wings for assistance. If something were to happen, the liability
for the city is too great. We hurl ourselves around in cars at
astonishing speeds, but we're not allowed to touch each other
crossing the street? It's an absurd arrangement, and by that I
mean when you lose someone, you see ironies everywhere that
the world does not allow you to talk about even half as much
as you'd like.

My father fell in the driveway the night after the accident. I
happened to see him as I was going up to bed. I called 911
and asked the dispatcher for a quiet ambulance, explaining
our house was on a street with small children and my father
seemed lucid and calm.

　　"It's probably his hip," I said. "He's ninety-one years old."

　　"A quiet ambulance?" she said.

　　"Just, no sirens."

　　She told me to keep him warm, so I took out a blanket.

"What were you doing?" I asked. "Why didn't you call out to me?"

"Looking at the moonlight." He lifted his chin. "Truth is, I'm tired of being the patient."

"I don't think of you that way." The words didn't sound right, so I knelt down next to him. "Thanks for getting the wreath for me."

He moved his hands in the gravel, clearing little patches of dirt.

"Holly," he said, "Mrs. Jones asked me to come see her night-blooming cereus."

"Mrs. Jones?"

He sighed. "One street over. White house on the corner? I was on my way home."

"Oh."

"It's a remarkable flower, huge and fragrant, and it only blooms for one night. She didn't want to be the only one to see it, you see."

I stood up. I could hear a siren in the distance.

"Holly," my father said, "if she'd asked you, would you have gone?"

"Mrs. Jones? I don't know her. To come see her flower?"

"But if she'd asked, would you have understood what she was asking?"

The ambulance cut the siren before turning down the street. Still, some of the neighbors came out and stood with folded arms in the blue and red flashing light. I saw a few children peeking out of windows.

As the medics lifted my father into the back, Janeen approached, one hand supporting her back, the universal sign of pregnancy.

"Is there anything we can do?" she asked.

Who did she mean, I wondered? Her and the other neighbors? Her and her unborn child?

"What would there be to do?" I said, and must have spoken too harshly because she looked offended.

"I don't know, Holly. I'm just trying to be a good neighbor."

"Ah," I said.

When a person on a bus exclaims "Oh, no!" or "Would you look at that!" and you suspect it's because she wants someone's, anyone's, attention—just a moment of the universe's time—but you lift your paper higher, or keep walking, not even granting eye contact, are you being a bad neighbor or just protecting yourself? I really want to know because I'm interested in what we can and can't do for each other. What is it fair to ask? Can you ask a grandmother to take down her wind chimes? An old man to come out at midnight to see your rare flower? A young family to empty their front lawn of plastic toys faded like candy in the rain?

Can you ask someone why she lives alone with her father? Where her missing mother is?

Here: One day my father swerved to miss a deer and hit a tree. It was a pin oak at the edge of town on a route they drove often. That's it, a simple story. They weren't arguing; they never argued. He wasn't drinking. No one's to blame. But we've never spoken of that day. Instead, my father devotes himself to a battalion of climbing roses over a trellis in his garden where her ashes are scattered, and I put a fresh wreath on the tree they hit as often as I can. You think I'm going to tell you that part? You think I'm going to tell you what it's like to put flowers on that tree? No. I am not.

So, tell me. If I clean his room and get him library books and make his bed and water his plants and clean out his refrigerator and do his grocery shopping, am I not taking good care of him? Am I not living with this disaster as well as I can?

But Janeen sits with my father, talks to him. It was not seeing the boy in the street that caused me to drive my car into the parked Lexus after my Wednesday burrito. It was seeing my neighbor put her arm around my father, who had walked on ahead while I talked longer with Leo. And by that I mean it was seeing the way my father leaned into her, a small collapse, as if he were bone tired and he knew she would support him. I knew they were friends. My father doesn't have a single progressive idea in his head about women and careers, but he enjoys talking to her about the books they've both read. Until that moment I didn't know how much the friendship mattered to him.

After his fall my father moved himself—temporarily, he says—to a rehabilitation facility in Richmond. He has a fractured hip and though he's on the mend, he says he needs a nurse's care and this will be easier. He found a place he liked, in part because of the well-landscaped grounds. I packed for him and drove him down there and have promised to visit every weekend until he decides to come home. Richmond is an hour away down the straight green corridor of I-64. I like the drive.

In the meantime, I am left with his garden. I must admit I had no idea how much he did out there until he wasn't around to do it. The summer was young when he left, but within a few weeks the trellis was dwarfed by tall, stalky weeds, Virginia creeper was choking the roses, and the small yard had gone to meadow. So much unwanted growth even though it's been dry. I've seen squirrels around town licking at damp sidewalks. I've also seen Janeen staring at the trellis from across the street, shaking her head. A few days later, I returned from work to find her fussing with the roses. Wearing a floppy sun hat and wielding shears, she was trying to restore order.

"I hope you don't mind," she said, straightening and putting that hand to her back. "I thought I'd be finished before you got home." She smiled and stretched. Then she pushed back her hat so I could see her eyes better. She'd worked up a sweat.

I never would have asked her to tend my father's roses, but if she wants to, shall I let her? Shall I tell her my mother's ashes are in each one? Would that be neighborly? I honestly don't know. But it feels too late for someone to arrive in a flurry of friendship and save me from myself. I'm part of a family in decline.

Was my mother a good neighbor? I wish I knew. I remember she had a habit of mirroring other people's gestures. In the evenings she would tell me and my father about her day, her head thrown back differently, or bouncing up on the balls of her feet in a way that was new, and you would know you were seeing a bit of someone she'd just met. Watching my pregnant neighbor finish her work with the roses, I put my hand on my back and wondered if my mother had done the same when she was carrying me.

"My father wants a bed of tulips put in," I said.

Janeen beamed. "I can help."

So now we're both getting something we want.

I'm a good driver, I really am. Yet I nicked a box turtle yesterday with my left front tire and sent him spinning into the ditch.

I'm sure I cracked his shell. I'd seen him with plenty of warning, even among the pine needles dried in masses like pelts all over the roads this time of year. I could have missed him, but I didn't and I'm pretty sure I'm going to do it again. And when my father's gone, I'm going to drive out of town and keep going. Maybe I'll ask Leo to come with me, by which I mean I'd like to see Mexico.

NEXT IN LINE

Bless the early risers, I say, as S and I pull into the CVS parking lot, for they open the buildings. It's a cool spring morning and S has been up since four thirty. We've read books, built towers, played with bubbles and crayons. Now it's seven thirty and, while S shows no sign of tiring, I am exhausted. Her father is asleep at home, and I'm happy for him. Tomorrow morning our roles will be reversed, a strategy I believe in even though it seems S is routinely sleepier on his mornings. He says he has the opposite impression, so clearly it's a subjective judgment and neither of us can be trusted.

I shop quickly. At the register, S starts howling when I take a box of sandwich bags away from her to be scanned. I try to set her down so I can pay the cashier, but she refuses to stand. She dangles her legs, suddenly useless little flaps of flesh with white sandals strapped to the ends. I dunk her a few times, but the flaps keep folding.

It's astonishing the number of customers in CVS at this hour.

The cashier finishes with the sandwich bags and I offer them to S. She grabs the box and hurls it into the air. It lands at the feet of a young boy, probably five or so, who, after a nod from his mother, picks it up and brings it back. He is speechless, in awe of S's passion.

"Why is she crying?" he asks.

"Well, she's tired," I say, although this is not really true.

He nods and returns to his mother. Even puts back the candy bar she doesn't want him to have. An angel boy.

I set S on the floor. In a sitting position, of course, but it doesn't last. She throws herself backward, flat on her back, screaming. She is directly at my feet, though, not abandoned on the floor ten feet away. This is important.

An older woman approaches, trim and well dressed in an elegant black linen pants suit. She's clucking her tongue and addressing S in soothing tones. "Don't cry, little girl. What's wrong? Oh, don't cry. It will only make it worse."

She moves close to S.

"Oh, little girl. Please stop crying. It will only make things worse."

S is still crying, but she has stopped screaming. She is watching the woman.

I'm ignoring everyone, simply trying to pay and get outside as fast as possible, but the tape in the register runs out and my cashier, with tricolored hair and a pierced midriff, is a trainee. She has to call the manager.

"I don't need a receipt," I say.

"Yeah, but, um, the register won't finish the transaction without the paper." Her name tag describes her as a "Convenience Specialist."

"How old is she?" the woman in black asks. She has straightened and is looking at me now. Her eyes are dark gray. I can barely make out the pupils.

"Almost fifteen months," I say, like the first-time mother I am. All my friends with second children just round up.

She turns back to S. "Well, tell your mommy you won't live to seventeen months if she keeps putting you on the floor like this."

And she reaches out and touches S on the forehead. She sweeps S's sweet blond hair off her temples.

I am horrified and, unfortunately, completely without words. Later, at home with H, I will think of many things I could have said, but in the store I simply swoop down, pick up S, plunk her back on my hip (where she stays now, thank God, the tantrum having passed), and complete my transaction. Almost everything I am buying is for S: apple juice, Goldfish, the box of sandwich bags (for her snacks), and a copy of *People* magazine (for me, it's true, to read during her nap). I'm embarrassed by the *People* and consider putting it back, but it's already in the bag.

"I'm just a fussy old lady," the woman says as I snatch the handles of my purse.

All I can manage is a "Yes, you certainly are," but I deliver it forcefully, a lot of emphasis on "certainly," and while I have no proof, I think the people in line behind me are sympathetic. I'm not the kind of person who usually thinks this way—I never used to believe in vibes and karma and positive or negative energy—but as I leave the store, I feel something I can only describe as a wave of support and good feeling from them. S, too, must have felt it. Smiling and hiccupping, she pressed her head into the crook of my neck.

I didn't know then it was too late.

It was the end of May, the beginning of summer, and I was taking S a lot of places. We liked the merry-go-round at Kohr

Brothers out on Route 29 and the brightly colored tables and chairs at Ben & Jerry's. Once a week we went to the public library downtown, where S enjoyed pulling many books off the shelves, but would not yet sit in my lap long enough to read a whole story. Still, her enthusiasm for books in general was a sight to behold and the librarians loved her. They issued her a card in her own name, and, if no one else was there, gave her rides around the children's section on one of the book carts. We joined a pool club in our neighborhood and went swimming often in the late afternoon. I've since asked the lifeguards about the chlorine levels. They shared with me all their paperwork for May and June, all the tests and water treatments and city inspection certificates. Everything was in order.

S was in her stroller less because she was walking so well, holding my hand, and I'd read somewhere that babies in America spend too much time in their strollers. We move them from car seat to stroller to high chair to crib. We push them through grocery stores in giant carts that look like cars. It's the beginning of the sedentary lifestyle that's killing us, and I was determined to break the pattern. So S walked a lot. Which might have meant that she touched more things than she should have.

On Friday, June 12, S woke up with a runny nose and a fever. By the afternoon, she was irritable, but H and I had seen this before and we weren't worried. All the next day the fever continued. So did the irritability, but overall I thought she was improving. On Sunday she seemed lethargic, stiff. She napped for an unprecedented four hours and when she woke up, she didn't want to move her head or neck. We called our doctor, who told us to meet her in the emergency room; there was an outbreak of meningitis.

I can still see the hands of the doctor who told us they

hadn't been able to save her. They were handsome hands, with round oiled nails. They rested in his lap, and he looked down at them while he spoke. We all looked down at them. I wish my memory of that moment was not crowded with those hands, but there they are, every time.

To be a woman in the world after the death of a child. How to explain this? It bears some resemblance, perhaps, to being newly married or newly pregnant. You are in a brand-new, all-encompassing state, and yet the rest of the world is oblivious. You have goose bumps and the rest of the world has never heard of them. You are nauseated and no one else even has a stomach. But when you're newly married, someone might see your ring, if you wear one, and offer congratulations. When you're newly pregnant, someone might notice the way your fingers flutter near your stomach, what you're suddenly not eating or not drinking, and ask.

Grief is solitary. If someone did notice your haunted gaze, the way you crane to see a baby seat in a passing car, the way you veer toward playgrounds just to watch, they would say nothing. They might assume you can't have children. You are completely alone.

I read somewhere that no man should call another man's prison term easy. War wounds, too, should never be compared. Add to these, I think, the loss of a child. And yet I think a lot about whether it would have been harder to lose her later. She was only a toddler. We only had a few clues about who she was. She liked ice cream and spicy sausage and lemon wedges. She moved her hands when she ate, as if she were conducting. She had a fine sense of balance and enjoyed crowds. She always moved to music. She laughed a lot. But wouldn't it be harder to lose someone you knew better? Is losing a toddler just losing a dream?

One day I spent several hours in S's crib. Later, when H asked if he could dismantle it, I didn't object.

Days passed, weeks, a couple of months. H went back to work. He got tenure. I don't know what I did. I read some books, I slept, I walked. I went out for coffee with friends. The coffee outing is unusual, I think. It's the visiting equivalent of the phone message—too brief to be truly intimate, just long enough to check in. My friends always suggested it and I didn't care. I find the planning and the ordering of a cup of coffee very comforting. I never enjoy the actual beverage as much as I think I'm going to, but it's nice to hold the warm mug. Once in a café with a friend I overheard another woman say to her girlfriend, "She's never happy. She's hilarious. God, she's one of my favorite people." Oh how we love our troubled friends! I thought I was beginning to fall into that category. When my friend and I were done I climbed back into my car, drove home, and went back to bed. No amount of caffeine could keep me awake.

My friends tried, they did, but none of them was up to the task. You could say my cast of friends lacks the truly exceptional, utterly devoted person who knows just what to do to pull you out of yourself. I've read about friendships like that, mostly in fiction, some in biography. Johnson had Mrs. Thrale, Boswell had Johnson. (Sort of. Johnson made reading lists for him, at least.) I don't know why this threesome comes to mind. In the novels of Anne Lamott there is always this sort of person, someone who rescues a friend from a tremendous gale of grief with a marathon TV-watching stint, or a blueberry crumble, or both. I avoid that kind of novel now. I don't think it's realistic.

Before S was born I was a journalist. I wrote a regular book column for a regional magazine and did freelance work for a number of national newspapers. When S arrived, I left the magazine but continued to freelance. Keeping my hand in the work and all that. Sounds silly to me now. After S was gone, I missed a few deadlines, and it was clear to me (if not yet to my editors) that I would be stopping altogether. Maybe a regular job would have helped me better manage my grief. I don't know. It was certainly suggested several times.

My walks were odd. I can only say that I began to see strange things. Or did I only begin to notice them? Maybe they were there before, as H says, and I just started noticing them because my spirits were low. (He always says "spirits"; it's a euphemism that helps him, just as referring to people by their initials helps me.) But it was an extraordinary run of things. One day while I was waiting at a bus stop, I saw the largest spider I've ever seen, the shape and length of a football, sort of stretched out along the curl of the gutter, four legs forward, four legs back. Another time, walking in the woods, I came upon a deer foreleg. No sign of the rest of the carcass. Did a hunter decide he didn't want it? Or was the deer hit by a car and the cleanup crew missed this one part? I went to the public library to read one afternoon and sat in the inner, enclosed courtyard. Suddenly a black bird flapped loudly in the square of sky overhead, as if it had been ambushed. It swooped precipitously, then hit a window and fell to the ground, dead, one wing up as if waving to me. I thought, *I am a magnet for distressing wildlife situations*, and started to cry.

The next afternoon from my desk at home I watched a hawk eating something he'd brought to a branch in the pine tree over our house. He was jabbing and tearing; I was on the phone with my mother, who was urging me to consider having another child. She had visited after S's death and been a surprising source of emotional strength. Now, however, she was losing me.

"Not that you're ready yet, Eva, I know, but you could be thinking about it."

". . ."

"Your sister was three before we had you. It seems wrong now—one child doesn't replace another—but at the time we thought we were having another child because we wouldn't be able to endure the loss of her."

". . ."

"And yet at the same time, you would have something left. You wouldn't be childless."

"So you're suggesting, Mom, that I have two more kids? Twins, maybe?"

"You're still so young."

Then, out the window, the hawk took off with his prey. That is when I remembered the woman at CVS. I was still at my desk and I looked at the calendar. S would have been seventeen months old in two days.

H used to say that CVS should stand for Come Visit Satan. This was when we were living in Washington, D.C., long before S died. He used to be very good at that sort of fanciful renaming. This nickname came about after he waited one night at the CVS prescription counter for half an hour, only to be told they wouldn't be able to fill his prescription because they didn't have all the ingredients. They actually suggested he go to Meadowbrook, a small, family-owned pharmacy across the street that they were slowly putting out of business. H snapped.

"Which part of your Service is this?" he shouted. "Convenience? I don't think so!" And he turned on his heel and left. I loved him for that kind of flair.

I started telling my woman-in-black CVS story to anyone who would listen. I would speak fast, fill in lots of detail. Did I mention the carpet was gray, the same dark gray as her eyes? And S was wearing a beautiful blue-and-white gingham dress that tied in the back. She was clean and fed. Her skin, where it was bare, was covered with sunblock. I was wearing dark blue capri-length pants, red sandals, and a white T-shirt. What did she see to make her decide I was an unfit mother?

Depending on how I'm feeling, I can make the story funny, sad, or threatening. There are lots of versions. If I'm talking to someone unlikely to believe S was visited by the angel of death in CVS, I can make it humorous, play up my impatience and the dumb cashier. If I'm talking to someone who, like me, realizes that something happened in the store that day that defies explanation—the woman touched S's forehead and S died of meningitis two weeks later—then I tone down the funny stuff and describe the real things, the things that haunt me. The way she said S wouldn't live to seventeen months and she didn't.

I've had a lot of conversations with H about this. He does not believe me, but he has nevertheless lost his daughter and is now worried he's losing his wife, so he's willing to engage.

The signs I point out to him: the dead tree in the row of dogwoods along the south wall of the building; the entrance, always smoky; the black pants suit she was wearing.

His replies: There's a dogwood blight affecting trees all over town; people are allowed to smoke outside the building; a black pants suit, while conservative, is not inherently evil.

I smile weakly.

But if the woman in the black pants suit was the angel of death, he continues, why did she bother pretending she cared about S's welfare? Why not just touch her forehead and walk away? And what about the other children who died of meningitis that summer? There were two. Did she visit them, too?

"Probably," I say. And then, "Wait a minute. 'S's welfare'? If you say it like that, aren't you implying that S's being on the floor was bad?"

"No, I'm not. I'm saying the woman in black thought it was bad. She didn't have to say anything at all if she was the angel of death, you see?"

"But do you think it was bad?"

"No." H shakes his head slowly. "A thousand times, no."

But after a bottle of wine, late at night, in whispers, we sometimes review our relatively cavalier attitude toward parenting. Cavalier. That's the cheerful word we used when S was alive and we thought we could eschew the culture of fear that consumes our contemporaries. It seems our generation is the first to admit that parenting is hard, and with this admission has come much liberation, but also much dread. Of failure. Of danger. Our children are too scheduled, too clean, too fat. In a way, perhaps, our children are too safe.

On the other hand, I put my daughter on the floor one day and then she died. Maybe H and I were fools to go against the tide, to try to hark back to a time when people didn't hire baby-proofing consultants for a thousand dollars, didn't secretly videotape babysitters and interview nursery schools.

"I don't believe in the angel of death, Eva," H says. "But

if you're asking me to think about this as if she did exist, then I will grant it's not that big a leap from there to imagine her going to CVS. In fact, she might be permanently employed there. At the pharmacy."

"I don't appreciate your humor."

"Eva?" he says.

"No. Not about this."

I consider CVS—and I spend a lot of time there now—a kind of secular gateway, a societal crossroads, not unlike drivers' ed in high school. Everyone needs toiletries, or a birthday card, or a pint of milk at one time or another. Some of its patrons have Gucci loafers in their closets, others have gnomes in their front yards. I know some families shop for everything at the Kmart out on 29, where the prices are lower, but even they can't resist CVS's holiday aisle, the center lane in most stores, running like a main artery through the body of American consumerism: Halloween costumes, Thanksgiving cornucopias, Christmas stockings, Valentine hearts, Easter baskets, Fourth of July beach balls, each season running into the next, leftover Peeps crowding the sunblock, cages of beach balls blocking the back-to-school pencils.

I haunt the aisles now. I spend a lot of time pretending to browse for cards or slipping baby pictures out of cheap wooden frames. Mostly I watch the mothers with children. I'm interested in anyone wearing black, too, of course, but I haven't seen her. The other day I saw a young woman—she couldn't have been more than twenty—with twins, one on each hip. These babies couldn't walk yet, so I was curious to see how she was going to handle her moment at the register. The three of them were underdressed. It was a cool, rainy day and the mother wore a miniskirt and tank top, her babies thin onesies. When you looked at the group, your first impression was of a lot of skin. She was buying a two-liter bottle of Diet Cherry Coke, which dangled from her long-nailed fingertips beneath one of her babies' bottoms. When she got to the counter, she pinned him between her stomach and a display of candy bars, paid over his head, snatched him up again, and was gone.

No one said anything to her.

Another time I listened to a woman talking to her three- or four-year-old son. While she was browsing for a get-well card, she told him he was bad and he was driving her crazy and he was going to get a spanking as soon as they got back to the car.

"I'm not mad at *you*," he said quietly.

Her eyes shot over to me. "Doesn't matter. I'm mad at you, Buster. You've got it coming."

I moved away, unwilling to provide her with an audience any longer. As I passed the boy, his head bowed in his stroller, I almost touched him.

No one said anything to her, either.

What about the handle of a grocery store cart? Or the common toys at the café downtown? Any playground, for that matter? What makes the floor of CVS more dangerous than these things?

S was not unappreciated, she was treasured. It's true: I was the kind of woman who considered conceiving a child simply a matter of course. But then I had a miscarriage at eight weeks. In another age I might never have known I was pregnant. The doctor seemed to sense I was not an emotional ruin, so he went on with the details. I would have some discomfort for a few days, he said, because blood was an irritant to all other tissues and substances in the body.

I nodded.

"Except other blood cells," he added with a smile.

I looked up. An interesting thing to say. Not so much hypertechnical as demonstrating an unusually fine sense of sympathy, I thought. In spite of the circumstances—I was half-undressed on a gurney, I'd just had a miscarriage—I found myself feeling happy for the blood cells. Good for them, I thought. They band together.

The whole experience made me more careful, more considerate. I cut all caffeine from my diet and began to go out of my way to congratulate pregnant strangers. When I conceived the baby that would be S, I was nervous, grateful. And when I passed eight weeks, ecstatic.

H says I'm engaging in "emotional alchemy," which he defines as changing an emotion into a cause. "You've changed your anger about S's death into a search for a woman who was rude to you in CVS."

"And was dressed completely in black. And touched S's forehead and predicted she would die. Why do you leave out the details?"

"Eva."

"I wish so much you'd been with me that day."

"Eva! You can't live like this."

"Why did she skip sixteen months? Have you thought about that? I told her S was fifteen months old and she skips right over sixteen and predicts her death before seventeen months. Which was, of course, accurate."

"I don't know. Look, what if CVS gets a restraining order? I'm surprised they haven't, actually."

"I'm very quiet, and I do not spend all my time there. I don't even go every day. Every other day or so."

We were eating dinner on our back patio. It was an unseasonably warm October night and H was exhausted. He had decided not to take the fall term off, one summer of grieving enough for him, I guess, but the strain of teaching, grieving (for he still was, I knew that in my better moments), and listening to his crazy wife was visible. He had a knot of muscle at the back of his neck that was giving him headaches for which he had started to take a prescription pain reliever. I could see him trying hard to think of a new angle on our problem, a new reason why it might not have been unreasonable for the woman in CVS, as he thought of her, to address S and me that day.

"Okay. S was small, right? What if the woman thought she was younger than she was, a baby who wasn't standing on her own yet? If she didn't see the scene developing, it would have been unsettling to come upon a child on the floor like that. Right?"

"She was wearing sandals. Babies who aren't walking don't wear shoes."

"Yes, they do. I saw a baby just the other day in blue sneakers and he couldn't have been more than six months old."

I looked at H. He looked down at his plate. We both knew he had just admitted to noticing babies as much as I did, something he had heretofore denied. Of course, I often went one step further, pointing out pacifiers on sidewalks, pregnant women several blocks away, and sweet family ensembles. Sometimes I pointed to less obvious things, objects that simply evoked childhood, a lost balloon floating above the trees, for example.

All I did was point. I never articulated my conclusions, but H knew me well.

We had finished eating, so I stood up and began clearing the table.

It was a very long winter.

Then, March. One night after an unimpressive snowstorm—the town looked as if it had been salted—H came to find me in CVS. He had not been in the store since S died. He never even parked near it. I had asked him why, but he wouldn't answer.

I was standing by the cold drinks.

"Eva, you have to decide to go on. With me. Or you can decide not to."

"Then what?"

"I don't know." He glanced around the store. "Live here, where they pad the poles with carpet. Is it a convenience store or a mental ward? What's that for?" He pointed to the padded pole.

My nose itched, but I didn't trust myself to speak. I shrugged.

H picked up a basket and headed toward cold remedies. He wasn't wearing gloves and his fingers were red and chapped, his shoulders hunched.

We browsed for a while, separately. I'm surprised we knew this was what we needed. Anyone observing us would not have known we were together. We picked up a few things. Me: Band-Aids, toothpaste, cold cream. H: aftershave, shampoo, Scotch tape. Gradually we drifted over to stationery. Without talking we picked out a birthday card for his brother, then wandered over to cleaning items and got a four-pack of the kind of kitchen sponge we both like. Finally we came to a stop with our baskets in front of the main counter, near the place where I'd put S on the floor. I stared at the carpet, then realized H didn't know where it had happened.

I pointed. I made a sort of circle with my finger to encompass the whole area. "I don't know what I'm waiting for. I just know I can't stop coming to this stupid place."

The film technician, a notoriously grumpy man, looked over at me and I lowered my voice. "Something happened here. I was careless or something. I put her down. I was mad at her."

H put his arms around me. I hadn't realized he was crying.

"At first, obviously, I wanted to see the woman again," I said into his shoulder. "I figured she must be local. But maybe she wasn't, maybe she was just visiting someone."

H held me tighter.

"And if I saw her now I probably still wouldn't know what to say." The admission hurt and I stood back and covered my mouth with my hand.

"I hate that," I whispered through my fingers. "It feels like I can't protect her. Can't? I didn't."

He started to speak, but I shook my head. I was getting close to something and I wanted to finish. "I think I come here to remember who I was. It's all so vivid, for some reason, what it was like to be her mother that day. I don't want to let it go."

He nodded and his shoulders sunk slightly. The weight of concession.

"But, Eva. You have to admit that the woman in black did not kill S. I agree you would have to avenge her death if she had. But she didn't."

He said this so seriously, I saw myself for a moment as an

avenger—long sword in hand—then felt laughter, one quick punch of it, the first in a long time. When I caught my breath, I said, "We just lost her."

"Yes."

I took his hand and we went to the register together. While H paid, I pressed my stomach against the counter, imagining the weight of a baby pinned there.

Last week I bought an anniversary card for H in the Encouragement section at CVS. We're going to go out for a drink and then see how we feel about dinner. On the front of the card is a picture of a cartoon mouse in a wan springtime scene planting a seedling. Above his head floats a dream: the seedling grown into a huge tree with wide branches and dense green leaves. Inside the card, the seedling reappears, so scrawny it reminded me of Charlie Brown's Christmas tree. The message: *hope springs eternal.* Just like that, in a careless lowercase that seems to belie the importance of the idea.

It feels less than optimistic for a seventh wedding anniversary. And yet I have hope. Ten days ago, on the first of May, I had what I can only call a visitation. Dozens and dozens of robins descended on the American holly in our front yard. They stayed for an hour, chattering and fluttering, and I sat on the porch and watched them. It was beautiful. I have no idea how some people go on from here to become counselors or start support groups or lobby Congress, but at least I'm sleeping less. And the other day I went to a park and realized it was the first place I'd walked after S died. With that, a subtle shift was complete: there was now a time after S was gone that was not the present. The world had changed again.

I bought H nothing else, only the card with its pale yellow envelope, the yellow matching a ribbon the mouse wears around his neck. And after I bought it, I left the store. I did not linger in the aisles.

My daughter's name was Susannah Jane. End of story.

THE STAND-IN

They discussed Job at dinner Sunday night. The divinity student, Adrian, unintentionally introduced the subject. He'd visited the Church of the Holy Sepulcher during the day and was shaky, spent.

"God does not ask us to endure more than we can," he said, his voice louder than he intended.

The dining room of the St. Andrew's Hotel was stone, enclosed and cool. The single large table was covered with a crisp white cloth. Breakfast was included, but if the guests wanted dinner they had to tell the proprietress, Irene, or sign the registry before they left in the morning. Irene did not have an assistant and served the meal family-style.

The girl—the guests had heard her father call her Hannah—took up the subject with more enthusiasm than any of them would have expected.

"But that is what has always bothered me."

Hannah's father, John, lowered his chin. "Always?"

"God didn't know how much Job could endure. Right?" Hannah said. "He was gambling."

At the end of the table, a couple from England arranged their forks on their plates.

Irene stood. "Shall we?"

The group moved into the sitting room, long and narrow, open to the Hinnom Valley on one side, the great stone entry hall and wide staircase of St. Andrew's on the other. The floor was white and all the furniture wicker, creaky in the heat.

"What you said," Hannah began when they were holding cups of tea, her voice low and steady. "What you said assumes that God knows how much we can endure and will not push us beyond that. But He was testing Job. Isn't the whole point of the story that it was a test?"

Adrian stared. He'd been a police officer in Glasgow before his calling to the church. Hannah was a teenager, pretty and privileged. What could she know of endurance?

Hannah appealed to Irene, who remained quiet.

Footsteps tapped and scuffed on the terrace—heels and a pair of comfortable shoes. A young couple appeared. They were also guests of St. Andrew's, but this was their last night and they'd eaten out. They stood with their backs to the group, gazing at Zion Gate in the distance, whispering.

John turned to Irene. "I'm not sure your theory of hot drinks works for me. I'm just getting hotter." He lifted his cup and smiled.

Irene took another sip.

Hannah lifted and tightened her ponytail. This was her first time traveling alone with her father, and she didn't understand why each night he seemed to engage with everyone but her.

"It's a good point you make," Adrian tried. "But perhaps"— he paused and looked at the ceiling—"perhaps we can't understand what God did and didn't know. That's what He tries to tell Job." He sipped his tea quickly and burned his tongue.

"Job's faith was being tested," Hannah said. "But for someone else, it might be something different." She looked at her father.

"I think we don't always understand everything," John said. "Especially when we're young."

The couple came inside and because they were handsome and obviously in love, everyone turned and smiled at them. A big man with sleepy eyes and a petite blond with an enormous engagement ring, they stood in front of the group and exchanged a few pleasantries about the day—So warm and sunny! Such an interesting country!—then went up to bed.

Irene said good night and went back to the kitchen. A few minutes later the guests heard a great quantity of mewing behind the door. When the sound subsided, Adrian tried once more to help Hannah.

"The Bible teaches us that when two or more are gathered in His name, He walks among us."

"Are we gathered in His name?" the Englishwoman said. "I mean, I didn't realize we'd be doing that." She smiled agreeably. "Was it in the brochure?"

Intended as a base for Presbyterian worship in Palestine, St. Andrew's was built by Scottish missionaries as a church and small dormitory in the early twentieth century. By the 1950s, missionaries fewer and money scarce, the dormitory had been converted into a small hotel. A pastor no longer lived at St. Andrew's, but the church was still consecrated and services were held twice a week. The guest rooms were large and clean, with soaring windows and high ceilings. The hotel had an excellent location, just across the Hinnom Valley from the Old City of Jerusalem, and was often full.

Hannah and her father waited in the lobby after breakfast the next morning. John had arranged a tour of the Old City with a private guide, a woman named Rosa he'd met the year before when, as now, he had spent a few days in Jerusalem after lecturing in Tel Aviv. He and Rosa had discovered several common interests—history, gardening, olive oil—and the following year they had exchanged a few letters. John sent Rosa a book of poetry she couldn't find; she sent him an Armenian tile to replace the one he'd broken on the way home.

Hannah hadn't known anything about the book or the tile; she'd first heard of Rosa on the drive down the coast from Haifa when her father shared their itinerary for the week. Hannah's mother, Elizabeth, was at home. About a year ago, with no precipitating cause anyone could pinpoint, she had simply taken to her bed. Hannah's father went about his life, albeit with a few more household responsibilities, and Hannah, baffled, had spent the months feeling the energy drain out of the house. This trip had been planned for her parents, but when the time came, her mother suggested that Hannah go instead.

She studied her father while he flipped through a guidebook. He was tan from their days in the north, and he looked very nice in linen. It was only his second time in the country and yet it seemed his wardrobe was perfect. Hannah had packed too few shirts, no linen, and her shoes were heavy for the heat. She wished he'd given her a little more guidance.

But when Rosa arrived she shook Hannah's hand and immediately complimented her on her skirt. Then she turned and kissed John's cheek. "I see you remembered pants this year."

John turned to Hannah and explained that last year he had packed only shorts, so that in a few places he had had to wear one of Rosa's shawls around his waist like a skirt.

"I always have them," Rosa said. "Just in case. So many tourists don't know how to dress for some of the holy sites."

"Let me see," Hannah said.

Rosa held open her bag and John picked out a pink and yellow shawl and swirled it around his waist with a flourish. "Ta da!"

Rosa laughed and grabbed the shawl back.

Looking back and forth between them, Hannah said, "Too bad you didn't take pictures."

Rosa had been an official guide for a number of years, she told Hannah as they walked, and now led tours only occasionally for family and friends. Slim and comfortably dressed, she wore no makeup, but her skin was radiant. She had a quick smile, spoke well, and seemed barely able to contain her enthusiasm for the city. She remembered a great deal about her tour last year with Hannah's father, mentioning it often as she explained what she would be showing them.

She led them first to a small market in the Jewish Quarter where they had some coffee and breakfast. "A locals' place," she whispered. They'd been together less than an hour, but they were an easy threesome. When they finished eating, John stopped in front of a stall of watercolors while Hannah and Rosa looked at some pottery.

"How old are you?" Rosa asked. "I have two boys. Ten and twelve."

"Seventeen. Your English is good."

"We used to live in New York."

Hannah scanned the table nearest to her. She picked up

a small blue pitcher. "My mom was supposed to be here, but she couldn't come. She's not well."

This was what Hannah had learned to say, though the truth was more complicated.

Rosa picked up another pitcher. "Can I recommend this one? It's a more characteristic style and the glaze isn't cracked."

Hannah took it and turned it around in her hands.

"I was wondering," Rosa said. "Does your father like spices? Do you think he'd like to see the spice market next?"

It was the sort of question her mother would answer if she were here, not anything Hannah had had to consider before. "Yes," she said carefully. "He loves spices. Especially curry."

"Good," Rosa said. She gestured to the pitcher Hannah was still holding. "Is it for you?" she asked. "Can I buy it for you?"

"No." Hannah said. "It's for my mom."

"Oh, of course," Rosa said. "I hope she feels better soon."

Hannah found her father studying a series of five watercolors, each a picture of a place in Jerusalem, not the well-known sights, but doorways, gates, small private gardens. The air was thick and warm, saturated with scents Hannah didn't recognize.

"Fifty shekels," the merchant said.

John looked patient and cool. He moved the watercolors, each the size of a greeting card, around the black cloth, as if trying to find their best arrangement. He held one up and turned it in a ray of light. "I understand that's what they're worth to you."

The merchant shook his head. "Fifty shekels."

John held another of the watercolors up to the light. "But the question is, how much are they worth to me?"

Hannah feigned interest in a crate of larger paintings against the counter. Bargaining made her nervous.

"Fifty shekels," the man said.

"Fifty shekels may be a fair price . . ."

The merchant raised his eyebrows, waiting. Hannah did the conversion; her father was quibbling over approximately fifteen dollars. She was surprised at him and flipped fast through the crate. His manner was completely new to her. Even his voice sounded different, the way he stressed the words *worth* and *me*.

". . . but they're not worth more than thirty to me."

The merchant exhaled loudly and muttered something in Hebrew. "Forty shekels," he said. "These are paintings, not trinkets, not"—he was at a loss for words and stopped to pull at his shirttails—"souvenirs," he sneered. He seemed to understand that John was with Rosa, who had come into the shop, and he turned to her. He spoke quickly in Hebrew.

Rosa laughed. "He says if you want toys I should take you to a toy store."

"I understand," John said, smiling as if he felt truly sorry. "These are beautiful paintings, much better than others of this kind. But, as I said, the important question is how much they are worth to me."

The merchant paced for a few moments, then threw up his hands and agreed to sell the paintings for thirty shekels. He wrapped them cheerfully. Before they left, he gave John his card and shook his hand.

Down the street, John turned to Rosa. "Well?"

"Very good!" She was beaming.

John looked at Hannah. "Last year Rosa was horrified when I bought something without even trying to bargain," he explained. "I didn't know how."

Hannah couldn't remember when she'd last seen him so happy. "Well, you've certainly got the hang of it now," she said.

"I'm not depressed," Hannah's mother often said. And, "You'll be fine without me." Hannah disagreed, but what choice did she have?

The anxiety of watching a parent retreat was not well documented. Hannah had searched books and movies, but the results were unsatisfying. It seemed that the child who stuck to hope and principles was always a coldhearted nuisance. The child who loved unconditionally, even to the point of laziness and harm—that child was the gentle hero.

"First stop," Rosa announced on their third day touring, "the Lutheran church. Its tower is one of the best places to get a view of the whole city." Hannah was sorry not to have more time alone with her father. She wasn't sure if she'd misunderstood in the car, or if he'd changed their plans, but it seemed Rosa was part of the trip now. When they arrived at the church, thirsty and hot, Rosa suggested John and Hannah take a break from the sun before climbing the steps.

"The acoustics are famous," she said, holding open the door. But John gestured for Rosa to step in front of him. "No, no. After you," she said, but John waited. They stood, smiling at each other. Finally Hannah stepped forward, but so did Rosa, so the two of them ended up squeezing through the door at the same time. Rosa laughed and rubbed Hannah's arm affectionately.

"Shall we sing?" Rosa said when they were sitting in the pews.

Hannah looked at her father. "We'll take your word for it," he said to Rosa.

"No. Sing," Rosa insisted. "It's really remarkable."

John shook his head.

"The hills are alive with the sound of music," Rosa sang in a husky alto. She couldn't remember the next words but bravely proceeded with *da da dums.*

Hannah studied Rosa's face. Was she wearing eyeliner and blush? It was hard to tell who was enjoying these days more, Rosa or her father. When Rosa stopped singing, John was smiling.

"Now you," Rosa said. "Really. Go on."

"We don't sing," Hannah said suddenly. "It's just not something our family does."

John shrugged and admitted it was true.

"How sad," Rosa said, and turned to face the front of the church.

They were silent a moment, then John opened his mouth and sang. Hannah didn't understand the words, but she recognized the melody of an aria from one of his favorite operas.

"What do you think of that?" he said to Hannah when he was done, breathless and amazed.

Rosa spoke before Hannah could. "Now you, Hannah! Go on!"

She called her mother before dinner on the pay phone in the lobby. The connection was surprisingly good, but Elizabeth sounded groggy, tired, though it was midday her time. She asked if they were having fun.

"Well, it's very interesting," Hannah said.

"How's your father?" her mother asked.

"Good."

"Making friends? He usually does."

"I think so," Hannah said. "You know, people like him."

"Yes. Well, he listens like a woman."

Hannah wasn't sure what this meant, or how her mother intended it.

That night Adrian was shaky again and looked unwell. He'd walked in the Hinnom Valley that afternoon, trying to find Hakeldama.

"Not very hospitable," Irene said, understanding his distress.

"No." Adrian shook his head. "Why is it not marked in any way?"

"What is—" began the Englishwoman.

"The place where Judas hanged himself," Irene answered.

"Some think it's the field he bought with the money he was paid for betraying Jesus," Adrian said.

"Thirty shekels," Hannah said.

Everyone looked at her. She'd had two years in a church youth group with a good teacher. Then she'd worked in the church nursery for a year. That was how she knew these things. She didn't know why it was so surprising to everyone.

"Funny," Hannah added, turning to her father. "Same as you paid for those watercolors today."

"But I am not a traitor!" John said, making a joke of it.

Irene began to clear.

The next night everyone at St. Andrew's was sunburned and tired. The English couple had traveled to Masada and seemed in the midst of an argument. Adrian had been back to the Church of the Holy Sepulcher and was in no better shape than the first time. Just as he'd felt close to inspiration, he'd been asked to take a picture of a woman and her father. Or husband, he couldn't tell. They both wore wedding rings, but the man was older and in a wheelchair. Adrian tried to refuse, but the woman pressed the camera into his hands.

John and Hannah had gone into the Judean Desert with Rosa to visit Ein Gedi. Rosa suggested they picnic at the base of the river, but John wanted to walk farther up. They walked for an hour, passing many lovely spots, all of them crowded with other bathers. Eventually Rosa began to tire, but John pressed on. So did Hannah, wanting to keep up, to impress him. When he finally veered off the path and waded into a small pool just below a waterfall, they were alone. They'd walked farther than anyone else and been rewarded with a spot all to themselves.

"I went to the movies," Irene announced. "But now I have a crook in my neck from sitting too close." She rubbed her shoulder.

John asked about the fish she'd made for dinner.

"Tilapia," Irene said. "I think it's better than flounder or sole."

"How do you prepare it?"

Irene paused, gauging his level of interest. "I simmer it in some white wine, a bit of garlic, fresh parsley."

John took a small notebook out of his breast pocket and she added, "Capers are also good. Do you cook?"

"No," Hannah said at the same time John said, "Yes."

They looked at each other. Hannah thought the circumstances of how her father had become a cook ought to be explained.

"My mother was the cook," she said. "She cooked all our meals. My father only started after she got sick." Her voice tapered off. "He taught himself. He's good at it."

Questions and good wishes came from around the table and Hannah let her father answer them all. She watched while he nodded and repeated quietly, "She's fine. Yes, at home. A number of ailments. No, fine, though." When Irene stood to clear, so did Hannah. "May I help?" she asked.

"An uncommon offer," Irene said. "All right."

In the kitchen, which Hannah was not surprised to find extremely organized and impeccably clean, Irene said, "There's only room for one. Let me finish and then I'll show you something."

Hannah waited in the doorway. A burst of voices came from the sitting room, where the group had moved to wait for tea. Hannah's father was telling a story. She could hear the familiar pattern of his voice and was pleased to hear the whole group laugh at something he said.

At the back of the kitchen, between two boxes of potatoes, Irene showed her a mother cat with four tiny black kittens. "I don't know how she got in," Irene said. "The tough little mama. I feed some of the alley cats on the back step, but this one got in somehow."

"What will you do with them?"

"I'll let her stay until the kittens are old enough to be moved."

"Then what?" The mother cat seemed thin and malnourished, but licked her paws while the little ones nursed.

Irene turned and started bringing in the bowls from the step. "They can't stay. I don't need an indoor cat."

Hannah tried to pet the mother, but the cat made a low sound in the back of her throat. "When the kittens are old enough to be on their own, what does the mother do?"

"Goes back to her old life, I suppose." Irene put the bowls in the sink. "I think she has an infection, though. Look at her eyes."

Hannah rested her chin on the edge of the box. "Would

you keep just one? You could call her Hannah. She'd be very smart and helpful and would never get in the way. I bet the guests would love her."

When Hannah carried the tea into the sitting room a little later, her father and the Englishwoman were deep in conversation. Standing with the tray at the edge of the room, Hannah watched him listening, his head inclined, nodding gently, and it occurred to her that her mother was right.

Hannah was sick of sightseeing, the stops and starts, the desires expressed as questions. *Anyone hungry? Should we go this way?* When they came to a balcony overlooking the Western Wall, Rosa said, "No one wants to go down, do they?"

To Hannah she said, "It's not known whether it is really part of the original temple. The only thing known for certain to be from the temple is a small stone pomegranate in the Israel Museum."

"That's it?" Hannah said.

Rosa smiled. "That's it."

It was midafternoon, the sun high overhead, the shadows of the people in the courtyard small puddles on the stone.

"Are we going down?" Hannah said. "No. I mean, I want to go down."

At the checkpoint, Rosa pulled out a shawl and draped it over Hannah's head and shoulders. John picked up a yarmulke and headed off to the side reserved for men.

"I'm going to wait here," Rosa whispered to Hannah. "If you want, the thing to do is write a prayer on a piece of paper and stick it in a crevice."

"I don't have any paper."

Rosa started to open her bag.

"No," Hannah said. "Thank you. I'm just going to look."

The courtyard was hot and bright and there was no room at the wall; women were praying there shoulder to shoulder. Intimidated by the wailing, keening mass, Hannah veered toward the divider, stepped up on a chair, and peeked over. In the crowd of men, most of them determined and efficient, as if executing a daily ritual, she found her father. He was bent over, using his thigh as a writing surface, scribbling quickly in his notebook. He was perspiring and seemed to lose patience when the page tore as he ripped it from the binding. The skin of his neck was loose, his hair thin. She thought she recognized the seasons of his life that were done and she grieved for him. He hesitated, then stepped forward and stuffed the paper into a nook chest high. As he walked away, he looked back to make sure it had stayed.

Hannah stepped down and turned to the part of the wall she was allowed to approach, tears filling her eyes. They were in a city where people made pilgrimages, where they came because they believed in miracles, and she couldn't even make sense of her father.

"Did you leave a prayer?" Rosa said when Hannah found her a few minutes later.

"No."

They stood side by side in the heat and prayer of the plaza. Hannah could smell Rosa's perfume and noticed she had a ribbon in her hair.

When John found them, Hannah slipped her arm into his and pulled him a few steps ahead. "I'm going back to the hotel now," she said quietly. "I'm tired."

"Yes, me too."

"No, it's all right, Dad. I'll go by myself."

"Are you feeling okay?"

"Yeah, just tired." Hannah looked down. "I thought you and Rosa might like to finish the day together. Rosa's great, Dad. I like her."

"What are you talking about?"

"If you and Rosa wanted some time alone—"

He stared at her blankly, and she realized she was going to have to say more. She took a breath and kept her voice low and calm, which was, to her surprise, mostly the way she felt. "She's interested in things, busy, motivated. You guys have a lot in common."

"What are you talking about?"

"Dad! She likes you and I thought you—"

He was shaking his head now, angry. "Don't be ridiculous."

"But, you can't . . ." Now her voice lost strength. She managed to say, "Dad, this is worth it to me. I want you to be happy," then stopped.

Her father looked away a moment, then back to her. "Hannah," he said. "You worry too much."

A laugh burst out of her. "Ha!" She rubbed her face with her hands. "What was your prayer at the wall? I saw you."

He smiled gently. "If I say, it won't come true."

"Prayers aren't like wishes."

He nodded. "That's probably true."

Hannah waited.

"I'm still not going to tell you," he said.

"You know, it's not fair for you to come here and behave this way."

"What way?"

"I don't know. Normal. Happy."

"But I'm not unhappy."

She shook her head. "I thought that was true, but then I saw you here."

"Now stop this."

"Dad. At home we never talk. We move around the house taking care of the chores, cooking. Here you tell stories, you're interested in everything."

She'd thought coming on this trip meant that something would be explained to her. She thought something *should* be explained. But her mother's absence had changed nothing at all. She had no greater understanding of why her mother was as disengaged with the world as her father was engaged, how they tolerated this difference, and what she was supposed to do about it.

"I love your mother very much, Hannah. You're very young. You don't know everything." He beckoned to Rosa, indicating that the conversation was over. "Now stop worrying," he said more gently.

Hannah watched Rosa approach. "But you're different here and I thought it meant something. I thought your prayer at the wall might have been for a solution."

"No," he breathed.

Rosa arrived with her big bag full of shawls, her easy smile. "Everything all right?" she asked.

"Yes. We're ready to head back," John said.

"All right," Rosa agreed. "But first, ice cream. I insist."

They made it to the ice cream shop, but had to wait in a long line. Only Rosa and John ordered, then ate outside on a bench in the sun. Watching Rosa watch her father eating the cone, Hannah wondered if she'd gotten at least that part right.

At dinner everyone talked furiously about what they'd done that day, where'd they been, how near or far away from a small bomb that had killed three people in the city that afternoon.

This was their last meal together at St. Andrew's, and the tragedy gave their gathering a significance they had not earned but gladly made their own.

Looking around the table, Irene listened to the stories— those specious souvenirs—they were beginning to tell. John and Hannah had been near the site just a few days before. The English couple had been there last week, shopping, and had noticed strange behavior. Did bombers survey a site before the event? A discussion ensued about whether this was likely, all of them suddenly thinking like terrorists, glum and formal. By the time Irene brought the tea to the sitting room, they were on to travel plans. John and Hannah were leaving in the morning; this had always been their plan. But the English couple had changed their itinerary and were leaving in the morning.

"We just don't feel safe," the Englishwoman said.

"What about you?" Irene asked, turning to Adrian. "Are you going, too?"

He shook his head.

"Good," Irene said.

John thanked Irene warmly for her hospitality and the others, rushing to be as gracious, chimed in. The sun was setting, the Sabbath was over, and the sounds of people coming out again to eat and shop filled the street. Irene looked at each of them, then said what she always did: "Godspeed."

Hannah's bag was all packed and ready beneath the window. Working in the dark, she found the ball of shirts with a small hard center and unwrapped the blue pitcher. She set it on the floor and sat with it a while. When she stood up, she wiped her eyes and pulled on a sweater. Downstairs she dialed home, but this time the line to her mother was hindered by bursts of a third voice breaking in. The interruptions were somber and unintelligible. They had the audio quality of a radio correspondent speaking from a faraway place and Hannah found herself compelled to listen.

"How are you?" her mother said.

"Okay."

"When's your flight tomorrow? Did you have a good time?"

The third voice spoke quickly in two staccato bursts.

"What?" Hannah said. The static was thick. Then, "We sang," Hannah said quickly, wondering if her mother would hear.

"Who did?"

"Dad. In a church with good acoustics."

"He sang? He used to whistle sometimes. Do you mean he whistled?"

"No."

"That's not like him."

"I know. He's happy here." Hannah waited, but her mother had nothing to say about that. Then Hannah asked what she always did, the question that perplexed her more than any other. "How are you?"

There was more static, then suddenly her mother's voice came through clear and sharp. "Is that what you want to know, Hannah? Is that really what you want to talk about? Because you know how I am, and I'd rather hear about your trip. Did you sing, too?"

But Hannah didn't know how to answer that question, and so the two women held the line in silence.

THE OLD BEGINNING

They had endured the deaths of parents, the divorces of friends. Turning to look out the window, John thought about all the summers he and Elizabeth had come to this house on the coast. They'd had countless meals at this table in the bay window overlooking the small yard with the little white gate leading to the sea beyond. Elizabeth had given him the stone turtle that sat among the silk African violets on the windowsill. He loved that turtle, the way one of its forelegs was lifted in mute determination. He couldn't understand how the same woman could have made such a suggestion.

"You're misunderstanding me," Elizabeth said again. "It's just not a bunny. That's all I meant. Of course it has a right to live."

"I think it might be a mole, Elizabeth."

He peeked over the edge of the shoebox on the table between them and watched the stunned, fast-breathing little gray ball. Her cat had caught it, the orange tomcat he hadn't wanted. Their first cat, Sidney, had been stumblingly aristocratic, a fluke of the gene pool, a farm cat with Siamese coloring. There was no kink in her tail, but she'd always held it very upright, as if there were. She'd died two years ago, at the age of nineteen, and he still sometimes missed the weight of her on his shoulder. She'd balanced there effortlessly, and yet often couldn't make the leap to the kitchen counter on her first try. Now they had Hodge, the marmalade lump. How Hodge, this doorstop of a cat, had managed to transform himself into a hunter their first morning on vacation was a mystery to John.

Elizabeth moved her coffee cup away from the box. "What are you going to do?"

"I don't know."

They'd never brought Sidney to the beach. They'd always left her in the basement of their house and asked a friend or neighbor to take care of her. Like so many things, this had seemed acceptable before their daughter, Hannah, left home, but was not acceptable now. Now, the cat came with them. Now, they owned two different cat carriers and drove twelve hours to their summer vacation with an open pan of cat litter in the trunk.

With his fork, he poked some holes in the cardboard lid.

"I don't think you have to do that," Elizabeth said. "I mean with a jar, yes. But a box isn't airtight."

"Okay."

He could tell from the way her eyes kept darting to the top of his forehead that something was wrong with his hair. He dutifully raised one hand to his head and smoothed the curls as best he could. Seeing she had his attention, Elizabeth sat straighter and raised her hand to her own head, showing him what to do. A familiar pantomime that nevertheless made them both smile.

He fit the lid over the box. He hoped the darkness might

calm the wounded creature. There was no visible damage, but when Hodge had deposited the thing at Elizabeth's feet it hadn't run away. And when she jabbed at it with her slippered toe, it had remained where it was, hunkered down, its head turned slightly, breathing fast. The sight had made him sick, and he'd started up from the table.

"Don't poke at it like that," he'd said.

"What am I supposed to do? Touch it?"

After locking Hodge in the sunroom off the kitchen ("Don't yell at him," Elizabeth called. "It's his nature to hunt!") he'd found the shoebox and scooped the thing up gently with a dustpan.

"I'll take it outside," he said and rubbed his eyes again. "Will you get dressed?"

Elizabeth nodded without looking at him.

"Okay. That would be good." He took a last sip of cold coffee and pushed himself up. This slow, conditional voice he used with her now made him feel heavy, but she often spent the whole day in bed. He hadn't meant to make the situation into a bargain, his handling of the injured animal for her getting dressed, but the morning seemed to offer no other choice.

Outside, he stood on the gravel drive wondering if he possessed the ability to kill this thing that was suffering. He wanted to put it out of its misery. But how was he supposed to do that? It was a mole, or a mouse, he really wasn't sure. Either way, it seemed preposterous to allow the situation to derail his whole day, his first morning by the water. He went back in the house and called the SPCA. Mole or mouse, it didn't matter, they couldn't take it. They were overburdened with family pets, the boy on the phone explained, cats and dogs abused and abandoned.

"What about rabbits?" John asked, staring at Elizabeth's

empty chair. She'd left the breakfast dishes and gone upstairs. John could hear Hodge sharpening his claws on the carpet in the sunroom.

Yes, they took rabbits. And ferrets. They had two of these now. Also, as of this morning, one fox with a broken leg.

As John stood in the kitchen, the phone pressed to his ear, his mind reeled with the picture of so much wild misery. He could hear the chaos of this ailing animal world, the barking and caterwauling behind the voice on the phone. Above him, Elizabeth was running water for a bath. He had the uncomfortable feeling that he was doing something wrong, that there was a relatively simple solution to this problem he just wasn't seeing.

The boy seemed to sense John's confusion. He knew of someone, he said, who took in wild animals and healed them, if possible, before releasing them. He gave John her address.

John cleared the table, washed the dishes, and wiped down the sink with a sponge. He swept the kitchen, then started upstairs to tell Elizabeth where he was going. Halfway up, he stopped on the landing and stood with his head bowed. There was no noise now coming from the bathroom, which meant Elizabeth's bath was drawn. She was probably already soaking. If he talked to her through the door, she would ask him to come in. If he refused, she would get angry; if he obliged, he knew he would not be able to look at her in the water with the love and desire she craved. He thought it best right now, when they had only just arrived for their vacation, to spare them this spectacle of themselves. He went back downstairs and wrote a note in the kitchen.

Outside again, John felt better. A wind was stirring, the air smelled of rain. This was his vacation and he wished for simplicity, another cup of coffee, the newspaper. He crouched, put the box on the ground, and lifted the lid. The gray ball was trembling. Its black eyes glistened, alert and aware.

It took a few days to open the house, a few more to close it up again. There was the drive, which John said was twelve hours but was really closer to sixteen. He liked to say they could leave at nine in the morning and be at the beach by nine at night, but in all the years they'd been making this drive, Elizabeth couldn't remember one in which they pulled into the driveway before midnight. John simply didn't think about the stops required for food, gas, bathrooms. All the effort hardly seemed worth it for two weeks of sun and sand. But John loved the house, and Elizabeth, bathed now and wrapped in a fresh cotton robe, was surprised to find herself feeling fond of it, too.

She was lying on the bed, on top of the quilt she'd cleaned and stored at the end of last summer. For a moment, everything seemed all right. There were two windows in the room and all that was visible to her was white and green: a white room, a white sky, and, to the left, a bit of the willow that stood next to the house. Its long green tendrils swayed in the wind. From time to time, a gust reached Elizabeth through the screens and she breathed the salty scent. She could hear the ocean, not a sound she craved as John did, but she found it soothing. John believed there was something about the sea, some atavistic need to be near water, that all people shared. Elizabeth used to smile when he said such things. Now she was likely to say she didn't feel that way and, in fact, had always preferred the mountains. These opinions generally made John uneasy and quiet, but after many years of a marriage in which she'd been the quiet one, the reversal thrilled her.

She looked around the room and remembered when the

house had smelled of mildew and there weren't enough sheets and towels and the mattresses were old and lumpy. It had been left to John by his father, who, in his last years, his health failing, had let the place deteriorate. It had required an enormous amount of work to get the place back in order. John and Hannah restored the back patio and repaired the small sailboat while Elizabeth replaced curtains and beds, sheets, pillows, and towels. It had not come naturally to her, keeping and decorating a summerhouse. She and John were not the kind of people who had ever expected to have one. Still, with time, it had come together nicely.

She smoothed her hands over the quilt, the tiny stitches like Braille beneath her fingers. The white cotton smelled pleasantly of rosemary and cedar, but her promise to John felt like a pool of cold water in her stomach. It should be easy to rise, dress, go downstairs, and yet she felt sluggish to the point of immobility, her physical strength as diminished as her will.

In the early years, John had arrived at the house in high spirits, a camper's or a soldier's sense of mission and adventure carrying him through the work of settling in. The first morning, after their late-night arrival, he would refer to Hannah as his assistant and promise her a trip for ice cream in the afternoon if she got her assignments squared away. Accustomed to her quiet, work-weary father, this new commander delighted Hannah. She giggled and played along, saluting him and running off to her tasks. Feeling slightly out of step, Elizabeth would leave them to the house, the boat, the survey and repair of patio furniture and beach toys, and go to buy the groceries.

Hannah came every summer when she was in college, but she'd graduated last year and was working in New York now. Her job allowed her only two weeks vacation. She'd come home for a week at Christmas, but the second week she wanted to spend with friends. Elizabeth understood this; John was struggling.

The house was quiet. He's gone out, she thought. She didn't know where. Something to do with the animal, she hoped, whatever it was. A car turned up the road and she held her breath. It passed and she exhaled. She longed for Hodge's warmth against her leg. He usually came running when she called, but not today.

This year John had arrived as tired as she. The drive was getting harder for him. She'd watched him shift uncomfortably in the driver's seat all day. And the fact that Hannah wasn't coming this year had him down. One night a few weeks ago, she'd said to him, "Don't you want to be there with just me?" and was surprised to sound more hurt than she felt.

"Of course," he said. "Of course. It's just different. Don't you feel that way?"

She did, but not as much. Their daughter brought out the best in John. She had fun with him and he came alive around her; the two of them joked and teased and laughed. Between Elizabeth and Hannah, the atmosphere was more solemn. Hannah talked earnestly of self-improvement, vitamins, books, exercise. She brought her candles and special teas. It was exhausting, all this evidence that she was not living the way Hannah wanted her to. No one problem ever came to the fore, but all the historic fault lines would yawn slightly. Hannah said everything was fine; Elizabeth wasn't sure. Their relationship was like a chalkboard that had been erased over and over again, but hadn't been washed clean in a very long time.

She called Hodge again. He had a quiet meow, more of a soft squeak that was at odds with his large body. She thought she might hear him downstairs somewhere. She rolled over on her side and stared at the white wall. When her eyes closed, she didn't notice. She was full of sleep.

"Would you like a drink?" John shifted in the doorway. He heard the edge in his voice, and tried again.

"Could I make you a drink, Elizabeth?"

She was on the bed, her robe fallen open. The room was hot and Elizabeth's hair was damp where it had matted against her forehead.

"Elizabeth," John said. She stirred and clutched at the quilt. She opened her eyes, slowly focused on John, and blinked.

"I'm going to have a drink," he said. "It's nearly six o'clock. Would you like one?"

"Yes. That would be nice." She sat up, pulling her robe closed with one hand, lifting the hair from her forehead with the other.

"Gin and tonic?"

"Okay."

"It's nice out," he said. The cool, stormy morning had turned bright and warm. "Why don't you come downstairs?"

Elizabeth nodded.

In the kitchen, he filled two glasses with ice, pleased that he'd thought to fill the trays that morning. He listened to Elizabeth pattering about overhead and wondered if she really would come down or if it would be another night when she asked him to bring her dinner up. Hannah used words like *enabling*, but it seemed to him a fine line between hurting and helping, enabling and simply taking care of.

When Elizabeth came down, she was in a pale blue sundress, her hair brushed, a bit of pink on her lips. She walked into the kitchen and stopped.

John could see she was trying. "Do you want a lime?" he asked. "You look nice."

"Do we have any?" She looked around the kitchen. "No."

"I thought you might go to the store," John said.

Elizabeth smoothed the dress around her waist and walked to the counter. She picked up John's note from the morning.

"Oh, I—" he said.

"You found someone to take the mole?"

"The SPCA recommended her."

"Did she think it would live?"

John poured the tonic into the glasses slowly. "The animal died before I got there."

"Oh. What did you do with it?"

"I'm surprised you're interested," he said. They were both watching his pouring.

"It's okay," he said. "I took care of it." He lifted the bottle and screwed the cap back on. "Shall we go out on the patio?"

Their backyard was a rectangle, a narrow lane to the sea. A small cement patio sat low against the house, two empty terra-cotta planters marking its far corners. Grass grew beyond the gate, but not well.

They sat at an angle to each other: Elizabeth in a patch of shade from the willow, John in the warm late sunshine. It was high tide, but from the low patio they couldn't see the line of waves hitting the shore. The grinding wail of a Jet Ski approached. This was safe ground; they both hated them. They turned to each other. "Terrible," Elizabeth said.

"Absolutely," said John. Hodge pawed at the screen door of the sunroom. "Can we let him out? He's been inside all day."

"No, not yet. I don't want him to run away."

Hodge's claws were stuck in the soft screening. "He's going to tear it," John said. Several streets away, a car alarm went off with a sound like a hovering spaceship. John looked up at the deep blue sky.

After a minute, Elizabeth stood. She pushed Hodge back and slid the inside glass door closed. "Someone's coming up the front walk," she said, looking through the house. "Oh dear. It's Max."

John lowered his face and rubbed his eyes. Max Lieber lived down the street. He was a year-round resident, their summer neighbor, and every year he tried too hard to make them feel welcome. He lived alone and seemed to have few friends. A couple of times John and Elizabeth had gone out for a drink in town and had seen Max sitting alone. John felt sorry for him, but he came to the beach for a vacation, which to him meant an escape from social obligation.

"Right on time," John said, and John and Elizabeth smiled at each other. Max was another burden they shared.

"You get the peanuts, I'll—" Elizabeth threw back the glass door with a flourish and Hodge ran out. "Oh!" she cried. She tried to close the door and caught the cat around the middle for a moment. "John, help," she said, but released the door and Hodge squirmed through. He ran low to the ground across the yard and hunkered down by the gate, his tail flicking back and forth.

"What do you want me to do?" John said.

"Nothing. Make Max a drink," she said.

Max had a small round head on top of a long neck. The effect, as he sat telling them about his difficult year, twisting and turning in his seat, was serpentlike. The sun sank and they drank gin and tonics and Max told them his business was failing. He led boat tours along the coast for tourists hoping to see dolphins, but the sightings were getting rarer and the tourists were more interested in parasailing and Jet Skis. Elizabeth found some mixed nuts in the pantry and brought them out unceremoniously in the tin. While he talked, Max ate small handfuls, each time brushing the nut dust from his palms as if not intending to have any more. Slowly, he was finishing the tin. John didn't like nuts, and Elizabeth took a small pile for herself and placed them on a napkin. She turned her chair slightly so that she could keep an eye on Hodge, who continued to slink around the yard.

"I'm sorry we don't have anything else to offer you, Max," Elizabeth said.

"Oh," Max started, chewing hurriedly, rubbing his hands vigorously on his legs.

"We arrived last night and haven't done the shopping yet." She looked at John.

"Can I get you another drink?" John asked.

"I'm sorry," Max said, swallowing. "I forgot to eat lunch. But I've already got something in the oven for dinner. Would you like to join me? I've got enough, I think . . ."

"We couldn't," John said.

"Another night," Elizabeth said.

A lightning bug appeared and Hodge leapt toward it, landing with a thud. "Not very graceful!" Elizabeth called. The bug flashed near the house, higher, and the cat leapt again.

Max was fond of cats, and he and Elizabeth began a lively discussion while John went inside to mix the drinks.

Standing at the kitchen window, John watched them. He could see part of Max's face and the back of Elizabeth's head. He could barely hear Max's voice; Elizabeth's was quite loud. He looked at the perspiration on the back of her neck, the way her heavy bottom strained the patio chair's plastic weaving.

He lifted his eyes and far up the beach saw the signal from a lighthouse. There were several along this stretch of coastline, but he couldn't remember their names.

When John rejoined them, Max was telling Elizabeth about a little girl he'd seen that morning. "She couldn't have been more than four or five. I didn't want to scare her, but I thought maybe I'd ask if she was okay. She seemed little to be out by herself so early. I stopped in front of her lawn and she looked over and said, 'It's my birthday.' That's all. She was wearing a party dress that was too small for her, white socks, shiny white shoes. The house was really ramshackle. There was a sapling in front decorated with those plastic eggs from Easter and Christmas lights still in the windows."

Max sighed. "I know I'm being gloomy, but I got the feeling something wasn't right."

John looked down and nodded.

"Why?" Elizabeth said suddenly. "A little girl up early on her birthday? She was excited. A party dress? Little girls love to dress up on their birthdays. The decorations may have been out-of-date, but someone put them up for her."

Max was nodding. "Of course, you could be right."

"But why tell a stranger it's your birthday?" John said.

"Because she's a little girl," said Elizabeth. "You've just forgotten," she said to John.

Max agreed. "But it was so early, and she was out by herself."

"She was in her own yard."

John saw the obstinacy in Elizabeth's face, and knew it was no use arguing. She would feel attacked if he continued to agree with Max, and the night would not end well. But her denial of the sad scene bothered him. Of all people, she should be able to recognize sadness and its ramifications. Annoyance blossomed in his chest, and he leaned forward for some nuts. Loath to eat them, he shook them vigorously in his hand.

Max started to stand. "It's getting late. I . . ."

"No, Max. Sit down. John's going to tell us what he's thinking."

"Elizabeth."

"Aren't you, John?"

Max stood again, this time getting to full height. "I really do have to go, but thank you both. See you soon." He walked himself into the dark yard and disappeared around the side of the house.

Elizabeth went inside, and John slowly ate the nuts in his hand.

"I'm very sorry," she said.

John had made dinner, and despite her insistence that she was not hungry, she had devoured the soup and canned vegetables he'd warmed on the stove.

"Thank you for getting Hodge in."

John nodded and ate in silence.

She considered how he'd become like a cat, preferring not to talk or be touched while he ate. Maybe this was their problem; Hannah's too. They were as aloof as cats.

John finished his dinner, then cleared their plates, washed them in the sink, and began to sweep the kitchen floor. Elizabeth remained at the table.

"Are you going to have coffee?" she asked.

"Not tonight."

"You always have coffee. I'll make it."

He smiled at the floor. "That would be a treat, but I don't feel like coffee right now. I'm tired." John put the broom away and stood before her.

"I'm going up," he said. "The doors are locked."

"Okay. Good night."

When he was at the stairs, she called to him.

With one foot already on the first step, he pivoted and stumbled slightly; a feint, she believed, to indicate the inconvenience. Still, he came. She lifted her face and they kissed. John even touched her shoulder as he turned.

"Are you coming up soon?" he asked.

"Yes, I think so. I'm tired."

They both pretended not to remember she'd slept most of the day.

Hodge went up with John, and for a time Elizabeth remained motionless at the table. When she was about to stand, a bird started singing near the house, a sudden, piercing sound that drew her outside.

The air was fragrant and cool. She searched the outline of the willow until she could just make out the bird's shape against the lighter sky. She didn't know what kind of bird it was or why it was singing at this late hour all alone. The song was loud, complicated, and wide-ranging, and for the first time in a long time she felt truly alert. Circling the tree, she thought she might stay up all night. Why not? Each new day required all the thoughts that disturbed her to be rolled away once more. She grabbed and shook one of the tree's long ropy tendrils. The bird stopped singing, and she imagined it looking down at her, its eyes bright seeds in the dark.

Yes! She would stay up all night. She would meet John in the morning, already awake, her day already under way. This never happened. It was always the other way around, leaving her feeling forever behind. She let go of the tree and walked around the house to the garage. She found the stepladder and brought it out to the yard where it would give her a commanding view of the beach and the sea; a fine perch for a night's vigil. Climbing to the top, she felt strong, better. She might even make the coffee in the morning. If she brewed it early, John would wake up to the smell—the sign, she'd always thought, of a house in order.

The cat and John lay awake in the bed, Hodge's paws kneading John's leg, almost painfully. When Elizabeth came up, he was going to tell her the truth: that morning he'd given the animal back to Hodge. The cat had finished it off in the sunroom, no mess at all, and now Hodge was devoted to him. John hoped this turn of affection would be short-lived because otherwise Elizabeth's feelings would be hurt and that hadn't been the point at all. Quite the opposite. He'd decided what she'd said about the cat was true—it was his nature to hunt. Giving Hodge the mole had been a kindness he could do for the cat she loved. And at the moment, that was the best he could do.

LOCAL BIRDS

John is sitting at the bar, drinking his favorite whiskey, watching his friends pretend this young woman, his daughter, Hannah, isn't a stranger to them. They didn't know her when she was growing up, and he didn't know their kids. In planning this party, Hannah has applied the customs of her child-rearing era to the past and made assumptions she shouldn't have. Nevertheless, here she is, looking beautiful and earnest, more interested in talking to this group of old professors, his colleagues of nearly forty years, than he is. He's glad to see her, and appreciative that she's flown in for his birthday, but he wishes it were a regular Friday night. He might have picked up a pizza and gone home to a movie with Elizabeth. Instead, they are at the fanciest restaurant in town, huddled around a too-trendy bar, waiting for their table.

"Your dad's a funny one," someone says. Barnes or Ellison, John isn't sure. He sees Hannah agree with a sad smile.

She orders a martini, which is a surprise. He's never seen her drink more than a glass of wine with a meal. She even knew how to order it: gin, straight up, with a twist. He imagines it's a good break for her to be away from her children for a few days. She raises the very full glass, spilling some of the drink over the edge, and makes a toast. The professors turn on their bar stools to listen. She says she knows he doesn't like surprises, but sometimes there are occasions in life when you have to let other people do things for you and this is one of them.

He frowns, but she continues.

She says it is a big birthday and that it seems like a good time to gather his friends because she knows he will refuse any kind of retirement party.

"You're correct," he interjects, and everyone laughs.

She nods and gestures as if to say "See? What can I do?" Then she finishes by saying that she loves him and has always been inspired by him. She wishes him many more happy years.

"Cheers!"

It's a festive group, everyone wearing warm fall colors. And yet Barnes's own daughter died of breast cancer not long ago, Ellison left his wife recently, Moore's wife is dying of emphysema, Larimer's old dog was just hit by a car, and Kossick has started having dizzy spells.

Thinking of these things, John's expression is grim, which doesn't match the occasion, he knows. Everyone is looking at him.

"People have been talking about this big birthday of mine for weeks," he says, "but I can assure you I don't feel a day older than yesterday." The group laughs again. He wasn't going to say anything more, but then he sees Hannah's face. Such love and expectation. So he adds, "It's nice to see all of you. Thanks to my daughter for planning such a surprise. She never did listen to me when she was growing up."

The group resumes talking on its own and the volume in the restaurant goes up a notch. Soon, he thinks, the waitress will come to take them to the table and the night will be one step closer to finished.

Elizabeth is sitting at a table next to the bar. He's astonished she's come at all, but she insisted, surprising Hannah, too. Just as it occurs to him he ought to check on her, he sees Hannah move to do it. Wonderful. This is perhaps the greatest surprise of his later years, the way his wife and daughter have come back together.

Elizabeth seems to be all right. Hannah brings her another glass of white wine. John asks the bartender for a glass of ice cubes, and then, his whiskey in the other hand, he walks over to Elizabeth.

"I brought you some ice," he says.

Elizabeth looks up and smiles. "Hannah remembered," she says. There are already two ice cubes floating in her wine. "She looks well, don't you think? She's having a good time."

He looks over at Hannah, who is speaking very seriously with Barnes, and wonders what they're talking about.

The waitress appears, beckoning them, and as the group hops off stools and begins to move toward the table, Ellison comes up on John's left.

"Your daughter's lovely," he says.

John nods.

"You never mentioned she was a writer."

"Didn't I?"

"She said she's happy to meet the other half of your life."

"Did she?"

The seating arrangement is going to be complicated. But apparently Hannah has thought of this, too.

"Mom, here, next to me," she is saying, directing people

with warm smiles, the martini finished or left at the bar, he doesn't know. His whiskey is gone; he orders another.

"Dad, you should be in the middle. Professor Moore, why don't you sit—"

It is all done very well and soon they are holding menus, though it feels very strange to John to be sitting at a table with his family and his colleagues. When he was Hannah's age, you had your family and you had your work and except for the occasional picnic or potluck they were largely spheres that didn't mix. Now, he knows, everything is all mixed up: you bring your family to work, you take work on vacation. Families eat out more, restaurants are always filled with children, two or three families eating together, whole tables of children wasting enormous quantities of food. But would the friendships last better than his had? Only time would tell.

Orders are placed and then comes a trembling moment when it isn't clear whether the table will converse as a whole or splinter into small groups. Ellison checks his phone, Barnes searches his pocket for something, Kossick excuses himself to go to the bathroom. John hopes Kossick isn't having a dizzy spell. Elizabeth looks uncomfortable and John begins to wonder if she will last through dinner or need to be taken home early. Hannah's attention is distracted by a boy at a neighboring table about the same age as her son.

The last time John saw his grandson they went fishing. His father-in-law was there, too, the last trip they had with him before he died. He flew up from Florida to visit them, all his fishing tackle confiscated at the airport because he had it as a carry-on. His father-in-law didn't even mention it until the third day; a lifetime's collection of lures, gone. If they'd known sooner they might have been able to do something, contact the airport, retrieve it. Even the seemingly heartless TSA agents would have saved a treasure like that for a few hours, wouldn't they? And yet John suspected he would have done the same, only explaining what had happened when it was mentioned, not able to bring it up himself out of some combination of pride and embarrassment and a genuine desire not to cause trouble of any kind.

He believed for a long time that this behavior would set an example for his family.

Elizabeth taps his arm. "The restaurant's busy. Dinner's going to take a while."

She is no longer enjoying herself. He doesn't know why, but that doesn't matter. He doesn't search for reasons anymore and is just as happy to help her make a smooth exit as he once would have been to figure out a way for her to stay. Hannah also senses a problem and is coming around to her mother's side after speaking to the waitress.

"What's wrong, Mom?"

"I need to go home."

"I'm sorry to hear that. Do you want me to call you a cab?"

Once upon a time Hannah would have searched for reasons, too, desperate to placate and include a mother who needed to remove herself. Now she is calm and helpful, a remarkable transformation. John wonders how she managed it. He thinks of all the times he might have intervened in the past, all the roads he might have gone down trying to negotiate between them during the difficult years. He believes not one of those roads would have led here, to this night, the three of them together. His mistake would have been to assume at any point that their problems were more than a stage. Everything is stages. He's glad he stayed out of it.

He kisses Elizabeth and says he'll see her later. "Are you all right?" she asks.

"Yes. I'm having fun."

Elizabeth looks skeptical, but then smiles. "Of course. Your daughter planned the party. Please," she adds. "If I'm asleep when you get home, wake me up."

"I will," John says and kisses her again as she ties her scarf.

Hannah walks her mother out, and John turns back to the table. He says, "I no longer trust the navigation of birds or the balance of cats."

It's a sentence he likes. He thought of it earlier that day when he saw a bird fly too close to an oncoming car. It was a brown-headed cowbird. He'd looked it up and learned it was an invasive species from the West. Apparently, it lays its eggs in the nests of other birds, jeopardizing the success of local songbirds. As for cats: he used to believe absolutely in their preternatural ability to balance, until Hannah's kitten fell off a banister when she moved into the house she's in now. The cat sustained a concussion and had to be given a shot of steroids. Currently its behavior is erratic and the vet blames the fall.

"Friends told me to keep him closed in a room until we'd finished the unpacking," Hannah told him over the phone. "But you've always had such faith in cats, so I did, too."

"That's interesting, John," Ellison says. "What does it mean?"

He meant it as an opening of some kind—really he just liked the sound of the words, but now his enthusiasm for it is gone. Here is Kossick, returning from the bathroom, looking pale and damp. John can't tell whether he has splashed water on his face or is sweating.

Hannah returns carrying a fresh martini. This one has a toothpick with olives, so perhaps she doesn't know what she's doing. She leans down to John's ear. "Mom says to bring her dinner home in a box."

"Okay—" he starts, but Hannah has caught the attention of the waitress and is telling her, too. The women laugh and then Hannah takes her mother's empty seat, sitting farther from John than she was before. The table is roughly divided between them now. He's got Ellison and Kossick at his end; she has Barnes, Moore, and Larimer.

Ellison is still checking his phone, so John turns to Kossick.

"John, happy birthday," Kossick says. "This is a very nice party, but I may have to leave early. I only ordered an appetizer." Of all John's colleagues, he is the most like John.

"Of course. I wish I could."

Kossick offers a sad smile. That's all John gets lately, sad smiles, as if they are the only kind left. The waitress brings a bread basket and refills their water glasses. John pours some of the water into his second whiskey. He will not be ordering another drink and he wants to make it last.

"Are you all right to get home?" John asks.

"Oh, I'm fine. It's just this damn dizziness. I suppose I'll have to see a doctor, find out what's going on. Must be my eyes."

"Let me know if there's anything I can do," he says, and Kossick nods while scooting his chair back. He's leaving now, that's what he is saying, John realizes. They were at the bar much longer than planned. He speaks to Hannah on his way out. Hannah looks quickly back at John, and when she sees that he knows, she stands and shakes Kossick's hand and kisses his cheek.

With only six, the already large table for eight feels vast.

John wonders if they ought to rearrange to close the gaps. But just then the food arrives and it doesn't seem worth the trouble. He puts Kossick's beet salad next to his plate. Someone—Hannah?—has ordered wine and the waitress is placing glasses while the sommelier opens the bottle.

"Dad," Hannah says, "Professor Barnes tells me—"

He doesn't hear the rest because Hannah is talking and simultaneously directing the sommelier to let him have the first taste. He swirls the glass quickly and takes a sip. "Fine," he says, judging a wine he didn't order, and the sommelier pours a perfectly equal amount into each glass.

Hannah is telling stories from her childhood, how she thought summer salary was summer "celery," how her father came to her elementary school to do science demonstrations when she was little, the time he warned the kids in the front row that it might be dangerous but not to worry, "we have ambulances waiting outside!" A couple of her friends had cried.

He likes listening to her, but she seems to switch from "dad" when she is talking to him, to "father" when she is telling a story about him. It gives his life a fairy-tale quality he doesn't recognize. He knows these stories, some of them have been repeated for years, but not these versions, exactly. The energy in her voice and the light in her eyes is new to him, and he suspects it is fueled by the cocktails. He glances around the table for the second, olive martini, but the glass is gone.

His friends are enjoying themselves, keeping Hannah talking with prompts and questions. Everyone wants information, it seems, about their family, the past. She folds her napkin delicately in her lap while she talks. ". . . my mom always said, 'I love you more than tongue can tell,' and for some reason, I pictured a hotel in a really desolate place at the base of a mountain. The slope of the mountain came right up to the side wall.

I always liked the words but at the same time not the picture in my mind."

She is lovely and animated but sharing too much, John thinks. Isn't she? Or is this just his perception? He is always more reserved than others.

"Yes, well," John says, "wasn't the second part of that 'and pencil and pen can write'"?

"Why do you think I became a writer?"

Ellison is smiling. Barnes, Moore, and Larimer fill their mouths quickly, driven by hunger or discomfort, John isn't sure. Not taking any chances, he decides to take control of the conversation and let Hannah eat for a bit. But what to talk about? Other than Hannah, they're all scientists, yet no one has had a working lab in years. They are all edging toward retirement, holding various administrative positions, but no longer supervising graduate students or running experiments. And that reminds him: Hannah told him once that when he spoke of "running" in the evenings when she was little, she didn't know he meant conducting an experiment. She thought he was actually running somewhere and hoped he would come back. She was always relieved to find him again in the morning. This makes him unspeakably sad. How could he not have known?

"Where's Kossick?" Ellison asks, as if just noticing he is gone. Ellison's phone is on the table next to his plate, so perhaps he really hadn't noticed.

"Not feeling well," John says.

There must be a script they're not following; John's sure of it. One in which conversation flows, ideas are discussed, and laughter instead of illness and regret reigns. They need a new topic, maybe an old favorite: the students and their behavior, the changing university. At one time each of his friends believed that one of the great advantages to being a professor was the way being around young people kept you young. Now, every year the students seem worse, texting in class, wearing flip-flops in winter, driving cars he and his colleagues could never afford. He's been to so many meetings to discuss the "fabric of cultural life on campus," he no longer knows what it means. But he often imagines it stretched tight and shimmering somewhere just above him.

Or maybe a new idea. He'd like to discuss a lecture he attended recently in the drama school. It was interesting and it had reminded him of the difference between modern and classical tragedy, which it feels good to repeat.

"In Aristotelian tragedy," John says, "the change of fortune from good to bad is not the result of any moral defect or flaw, but a mistake of some kind that the hero could not foresee."

Cats do fall, birds do die on the side of the road, he thinks.

"A mistake," Hannah says, nodding.

"Yes. I like that narrow definition. Modern tragedy is just about everything else, of course."

No one at the table is as interested as he and Hannah.

"John, what else are you doing to celebrate your birthday?" This from Barnes, who nursed his daughter in her final days because she didn't have a husband and her mother died years ago. Not a tragedy by classical standards.

"Oh, this is more than enough for our family," John says.

"It's true," Hannah agrees. "We're not really celebrators. But I'm staying around for a few days."

"Which is very nice," John says. "I'm looking forward to that."

The waitress clears their plates and winks at Hannah and suddenly a small chocolate cake is being carried out and his friends are singing. Hannah starts them off and the pace is too slow so that the tune feels more downbeat than it's meant to. He blows out the single candle—Hannah cries, "I hope you made a wish!"—and then the waitress moves in to cut and serve. Hannah has ordered coffee, which everyone gladly accepts, and the cake is very good. For a few minutes, they all eat in silence.

The families with children have gone and the restaurant is quieter now, full of small parties of adults. It's homecoming weekend at the local high school and there are several young couples in fancy dresses and tuxedos. It seems to him they have a greater sense of style than he remembers having, or Hannah having, at the same age. Probably it's all the movies and TV. Someone behind John says, "Do you think we're going to get through this without crying?" and he turns in his seat to see two middle-aged women having dinner together, no one he knows, but there's a small wrapped package on the table so they must be celebrating something, too. He silently wishes them luck and turns back around.

Hannah returns from the bathroom and the good-byes begin. This is the moment he longed for at the beginning of the evening, and yet he feels a little melancholy now that it has come. He shakes hands with his friends; he has never done anything else. His daughter hugs all of them and kisses their cheeks. He hears her say, "You've just known my father for so long—" She's a little unsteady on her feet, but still smiling.

They put on coats and say they'll see each other soon, but in truth, he doesn't know when he will next see them. For god's sake, Moore is fully retired and spends half the year in Florida. It's not like the days when they were all teaching and had offices along the same hall. John feels a pressure in his chest he recognizes. He worries that the weight of accumulated memory will one day suffocate him for good. How is he supposed to get any older?

"Dad," says Hannah, an urgency to her voice. "I'm sorry, I've got to run outside. I think I'm going to be sick. Will you pay and I'll pay you back? I never meant for you to pay."

"Of course. I'll be right out. I'll meet you by the car."

John gets the bill and pays quickly. He is sorry the night is ending this way for Hannah. As he steps away from the table, he stops and looks back. This is his habit, from years of traveling. He gathers himself and his things, takes a few steps, then turns to make sure he hasn't left anything behind.

It surprises him how often he does forget something, and not just the most obvious things like sunglasses or a pair of gloves, but also gifts he's bought or tickets for the very thing he is planning to do next. The tendency to leave things behind is his only weakness as a traveler. But now he is home, in the town where he has lived and worked for forty years, and as he looks back and pats his jacket lapel and makes sure his wallet is in his back pocket, he can't shake the feeling that there is something out of place, or something he has forgotten. Exit, pursued by a bear, he thinks, pleased to remember Shakespeare at a time like this, and goes out to find his daughter.

ACKNOWLEDGMENTS

I'd like to thank the MacDowell Colony and the Virginia Center for the Creative Arts for fellowships that allowed me to start and finish some of these stories. I'm very grateful to the editors of the magazines where a number of them were first published: *Brain, Child, Five Chapters,* the *Missouri Review, Narrative, Post Road, Swink,* the *Yale Review,* and *A Public Space.* My deepest thanks to everyone at Graywolf Press, especially Fiona McCrae and Katie Dublinski, who both thought about this collection as hard as I did. I'd also like to thank Portobello Books in the UK for remaining enthusiastic supporters, especially my editor, Laura Barber.

Jessica Francis Kane is the author of a story collection, *Bending Heaven*, and a novel, *The Report*, which was a Barnes & Noble "Discover Great New Writers" selection and a finalist for the Center for Fiction's 2010 Flaherty-Dunnan First Novel Prize, the Indie Booksellers' Choice Award, and the Grub Street Book Prize for Fiction. It is currently being adapted for the stage and the screen. Her stories and essays have appeared in *Virginia Quarterly Review*, the *Missouri Review*, *Granta*, *Narrative*, *McSweeney's*, the *Yale Review*, *A Public Space*, *Salon*, the *Millions*, and elsewhere. She is the recipient of fellowships from the MacDowell Colony and the Virginia Center for the Creative Arts. A contributing writer for the online magazine the *Morning News*, she lives with her family in New York City.

This Close is typeset in Palatino, a font based on the humanist fonts of the Italian Renaissance, which mirror the letters formed by a broad nib pen. Composition by BookMobile Design and Digital Publisher Services, Minneapolis, Minnesota. Manufactured by Versa Press on acid-free 30 percent postconsumer wastepaper.